BODY BLOW

A John Rockne Mystery

DAN AMES

BODY BLOW

A John Rockne Mystery

by

Dan Ames

FOREWORD

Do you want more killer crime fiction, along with the chance to win free books? Then sign up for the DAN AMES READER GROUP at:

AuthorDanAmes.com

BODY BLOW

A John Rockne Mystery

by

Dan Ames

"Where there is only a choice between cowardice and violence, I would advise violence."
— *Mahatma Gandhi*

CHAPTER ONE

They used to call him Dynamite.

Billy "Dynamite" Dawkins from Detroit.

Pound for pound, one of the most ferocious light heavy-weights of all time. Each fist was a bundle of high-powered explosive, ready to detonate along the chin or body of every opponent he faced.

The logo they'd used was a pair of hands, each wearing a boxing glove, holding a stick of dynamite.

Now, the man known for some of the most vicious punches and body shots in boxing history, was having trouble threading fishing line through the eye of a lure.

"Damnit," he said.

The sun hung directly overhead. Another gorgeous summer day in Good Isle, Michigan, a picturesque commu-nity along the northwest shore of the state's lower peninsula. Lake Michigan was a deep blue but when it reached the shal-lows, the water became beautifully clear and almost Caribbean blue.

Dawkins squinted and finally managed to fit the line through the lure's tiny opening, and he quickly tied a fisherman's knot. He already had one bait in the water, a lively chub minnow that was probably exhausting itself trying to break free.

Fishing with a lure from the Good Isle pier didn't make a lot of sense.

It was too late for smallmouth, too early for the big pike that sometimes moved in. That didn't matter too much to Dawkins. He was just happy to be out in the sun on a beautiful day, not sweating it out in some dark, damp gym that smelled like a bunch of men who hadn't bathed in weeks.

He cast the lure and varied his retrieve, bouncing it along the rocky bottom, lifting his rod tip to bring it up over a small weed bed he'd been able to vaguely make out.

Nothing.

The line with his live bait had moved under the pier so Dawkins cast out his lure again, a long arcing heave that landed a good thirty yards from the pier.

He set the pole down and picked up his line with the live bait, but he knew the minute he did so that the chub was gone. It had either worked its way free or been chewed off nimbly by some small fish.

He brought the rig back in, fastened the empty hook to one of the guides on the rod and set it down. He picked up the pole with the lure and reeled in until it suddenly stopped in his hand. His hope for a bite quickly diminished as he realized he was snagged. He pulled, and his rod bent nearly in half before popping free. The line was completely slack.

Another seven dollar fishing lure donated to Lake Michigan.

He reeled in the rest of his line, picked up his other pole and tackle box, and headed back to his vehicle.

His tennis shoes thudded softly on the dock's wooden boards. Children's laughter reached his ears and he saw a small group of kids with a woman by the ice cream stand, near the bathrooms.

A large sailboat nosed its way into the marina, a woman in white shorts and a pink polo shirt stood ready to help guide the boat into its slip.

Dawkins walked toward his vehicle, thinking about the morning. He had only caught one fish, and it had been a carp, which he'd dumped back into the lake. He hated carp and would have preferred to throw it on the bank, but the pier stuck out into the middle of the lake and he had no way of disposing of the trash fish. So he'd reluctantly let it go.

Tonight, if he wanted to have fish for dinner, he'd have to get it the old-fashioned way. At the grocery store.

Doing the math in his head, he realized that if he'd just gone to the store and bought a filet, instead of losing his lure, he would've been even right about now.

As someone told him once, that's why they call it fishing and not catching.

Dawkins got to the parking lot and his mood immediately lifted. His vehicle was a lovingly restored Ford Bronco, over thirty years old. It was his pride and joy and every time he looked at it, he felt a sense of satisfaction. So much of his professional life had been on the road, riding in other people's vehicles, that when he'd finally called it quits on his career, having his own car had been an unexpected pleasure.

Now, as he reached his SUV, Dawkins went to the back, unlocked the latch, and lifted the rear window, and then lowered the tailgate.

He would stow his gear, and maybe stop at the diner downtown for lunch.

A sudden sharp, stabbing pain between his shoulder blades made him jump.

Goddamn bees, he thought.

He dropped his fishing pole and tackle box, reached back

to feel where the bee had stung him, and his fingers found a small dart protruding from his back.

His vision became fuzzy and he felt faint.

Dawkins put a hand out to steady himself but he was suddenly shoved forward and he felt himself being lifted into the back of his vehicle.

Darkness overtook him as he heard the tailgate being slammed shut.

CHAPTER TWO

It's not easy telling parents that their son is a thief.

I knew that firsthand because I was just about to do exactly that.

Eugene and Laurie Weborg were the proud parents of two children. Katie was a senior in high school at Grosse Pointe South.

The other child's name was James.

James had been spending a fair amount of money recently and since he didn't have a job, his parents had become suspicious about how exactly he was buying a Rolex watch and expensive artwork hanging in his bedroom.

Laurie was a friend of Anna, my wife, and so they hired me to look into it.

James was several years older than his sister, but had dropped out of college and was living at home. I'd never met him, but the Weborgs showed me some pictures of him and he was a good-looking young man who looked like he had a bright future in front of him.

After being officially hired, I followed James and it turned out that he had a very good friend who lived in one of the monstrously big, expensive homes in Grosse Pointe Farms and James spent an awful lot of time with the family.

And not only did he spend a lot of time with the family, I noticed that he rarely left the house empty-handed. Often times there was a bag, box, or briefcase that he left with but that he hadn't been carrying when he arrived.

I knew that James often visited the family when his friend wasn't even there and that he had obviously befriended the elderly parents.

Finally, I noticed that James had his own unit at a self-storage facility in St. Clair Shores.

I followed him, and used binoculars to see that he had his own little treasure trove of antiques. I saw artwork and even furniture.

As an investigator, one should never jump to conclusions, but I strongly suspected that James was simply stealing from his friend's family. The next time he visited his friend's family, I used a camera with a high-powered lens to document his outing. First, going into the house empty-handed. Second, leaving with an object, in this case, framed artwork. Finally, his arrival at the storage unit, where he placed his new acquisition among the others.

Additionally, I was able to track James as he took one of the objects directly to a pawn shop in Detroit and sold it for cash.

So now I was faced with telling Eugene and Laurie that the evidence quite clearly showed their son was a thief. Of course, final proof meant getting into the storage unit, documenting what was inside, and then contacting the friend and his family to corroborate the items were, indeed, stolen.

That would require the Weborgs to take over. Or, it meant I would have to contact the police.

As always I decided breaking bad news with humor was the best route.

"I'm a big Rolling Stones fan and you know what my favorite album of theirs is?"

The Weborgs looked at me with blank expressions.

"Sticky Fingers."

Realization dawned on Laurie's face while Eugene continued to wear an expression of skeptical indifference.

"Your son is most likely a thief," I said, to clearly get the point across to Eugene.

This time Laurie gasped and Eugene's face turned red.

"I'm sorry to be so blunt about it," I said. "But there's just no way around it."

"I'm going to kill that little piece of shit," Eugene growled.

"Are you sure?" Laurie asked me. I detailed my investigation, and showed them the photos of James stockpiling his loot in the storage unit.

"Technically, as a PI, I'm supposed to report crime to the police, but I think this is something that can probably be handled between the families," I said.

Eugene's jaw jutted out. "That's right," he said. "We'll take care of this." He turned to his wife. "Cut him his check."

He glared back at me.

"I don't want to hear from you ever again on this matter," he said.

"Don't shoot the messenger," I said.

Laurie slid a check across the desk to me and I saw she had added a bonus.

They left, with Eugene giving my door a nice slam on the way out.

I signed the check, and then used my phone to take a picture of its front and back and deposited it into my business checking account through my bank's app.

Closing a case always gave me a good feeling, especially when money landed in my account. It was time to close up the office and head home, see if Anna had made pasta. I was hungry.

My phone rang and I considered ignoring it, but then saw that it was my sister, Ellen, also known as the Grosse Pointe Chief of Police.

"No thank you," I said, after picking up my phone and connecting. "I don't want to buy any of your Mary Kay Cosmetics."

"Really? I would think you'd like to buy a lot of my wrinkle concealer," Ellen said. "You're aging faster than the overripe bananas in my kitchen."

"Not needed, thanks to my youthful exuberance," I pointed out.

"That and your pre-adolescent sense of humor."

I looked at the clock and thought about Anna's pasta. My tummy growled a little bit.

"Do you have a dog in your office?" Ellen asked.

"No, I'm just hungry," I said, a bit annoyed that she had been able to hear it. "So what do I owe the pleasure of this phone call? As enjoyable as it always is."

"Ever hear of a town called Good Isle?"

"Sure," I said. "I've even been there once. It's a little town up north, right on the lake? Right?"

"Yep." There was a pause and then she said without her usual snarky tone of voice, "It turns out they're looking for a new police chief and they invited me up to talk about it."

That stopped me in my tracks and visions of Anna's pasta left my head.

"Are you kidding me?" I said. "You're leaving Grosse Pointe? Since when were you thinking of doing this?"

"I wasn't, really. Until they called me."

To be honest, despite all the times we've joked and made fun of each other, I couldn't imagine not having Ellen around Grosse Pointe. Both personally and professionally.

"But that's not why I called," she said. "When they booked my room they actually reserved two rooms and I have them for the weekend. I wondered if you and Anna and the kids wanted to come up and join me. It's supposed to be a beautiful weekend, sunny and it's a free place to stay. Plus, I know you never take your wife anywhere."

I thought about it and although I wasn't always up-to-date on the Rockne social calendar, I didn't think we had any obligations for the weekend.

"Tell you what," I replied. "I'll talk to the boss at home but I would love to come up north for a long weekend, even if you're there."

"Okay let me know," she said. "It might be fun, especially if only Anna and the kids come."

"Good luck with the interview," I said. And even I had to admit that I hadn't said it with any kind of enthusiasm.

CHAPTER THREE

Ellen Rockne strolled down the main street of Good Isle, Michigan and breathed in the crisp, cool air.

She was glad the interview was over, even though she thought it had gone quite well. There'd been the usual suspects: the mayor, city commissioner other city council members. They'd also included one of the long-standing deputies.

The questions were mundane and everything she'd expected and prepared for. She mostly came up here because she figured she was getting a free weekend up north away from Grosse Pointe.

Apparently, her name had been given by a Gross Pointer who had moved up to retire and who was a friend of Good Isle's mayor.

When the chief of police had been forcibly removed, Ellen's name had been given to the mayor. She still hadn't gotten the full story behind the former chief's dismissal, but her curiosity was definitely aroused.

One thing led to another and now she had just completed

a two-hour interview for chief of police of Good Isle, Michigan.

Afterward, she had thanked everyone for their time, nodded when they said they would get back to her, and left. She had driven to the small downtown and parked.

Now, she continued to stroll and occasionally looked into shop windows where she saw a curious mix of high fashion and sporting goods.

At one point, she caught her reflection in the widow of a furniture store. She had dressed casually, but she was in good shape. Still young, she had short brown hair, a lean face that could appear sharp at times, and friendly blue eyes that could go cold in an instant.

Ellen usually downplayed her looks in her line of work, but for the interview she'd gone with a little bit of makeup.

Dressing down could become a habit, and she only realized it on those rare occasions when she had to do the opposite.

She continued walking, all the while the stunning blue of Lake Michigan was off to her left. And a high bluff, covered in pine trees, was to the right.

The town was picture-postcard beautiful.

And suddenly Ellen found herself seriously considering the job.

She had to admit, she was tired of Grosse Pointe. There, she said it. She was tired of the small community right next to Detroit. Yes, she had a lot of friends and she had her brother and his family.

There was a history with Grosse Pointe, a comfort level that was undeniable. She also liked Grosse Pointe's neighbor, Detroit. The city had experienced a major comeback in recent years and was now becoming home to more and more cool restaurants and bars.

Sure, there was still no shortage of crime, but the city looked nothing like it had ten years ago.

Ellen wondered if she simply needed a break and that's why she was suddenly considering a move.

The fact was, being in law enforcement in Grosse Pointe presented its own unique challenges. And as beautiful a city Grosse Pointe was, she got tired of the constant policing that involves being next to one of the most dangerous cities in the world.

Nothing against the city of Detroit, it had its own unique charms. But she had to face facts she was no longer necessarily a spring chicken. She was not involved with anyone at the moment, and her last serious relationship had been years ago.

Ellen had never even really considered moving up north. But Good Isle was a fantastic, beautiful town. Yes, she was not naïve. She knew that even small towns could be snake pits when it came to politics. As bad, or even worse, than big cities.

What was that saying about the devil you knew?

She checked her phone.

The man who had recommended her, Beau Gordon, had invited her for a quick cup of coffee after the interview.

Now, she spotted the sign for Black Bear Coffee and popped inside.

"Ellen!"

The man sitting at a table with a copy of the local newspaper by his side stood and gave Ellen a hug. Beau Gordon was a big man, a retired attorney with a passion for sailboats and blondes. He had finally settled on a wife, his fourth, and the town of Good Isle.

His thick, silver hair was brushed back neatly, and he wore blue jeans with a crisp yellow shirt and boat shoes.

"How did it go?" he asked her.

"I thought it went well, but you never really know," Ellen answered. She ordered a coffee and joined Beau at his table.

Ellen only knew Beau a little bit, as he'd been a friend of the family. But she had come in contact with him when he was on the city council of Grosse Pointe. There, they had gotten to know each other, professionally, and he had been an ally of hers.

"They'd be crazy not to hire you," Beau said. "But that's the thing about small towns like Grosse Pointe, and Good Isle, for that matter. Small towns have a lot of backward people for whom common sense just doesn't apply. I can't guarantee anything, but I told them they would be morons not to consider you."

"Well, I appreciate it, Beau," Ellen said.

"What do you think of the town?"

"It's beautiful, of course," Ellen said. "Then again, it isn't February."

Winters could be tough in northern Michigan, no doubt about it. But Ellen enjoyed a lot of outdoor winter activities like ice skating, snowmobiling, snowshoeing and cross-country skiing.

"That's true," he said. "You get used to it, I guess. Plus, I've got a condo in Florida I go to for three months in winter. Helps break up the monotony."

Ellen asked him about his wife, and their grown children. Eventually, they finished their coffee and continued to walk up the street until Beau turned and stuck out his hand.

"It was great to see you again, Ellen," he said. His eyes narrowed slightly. "How is John doing?"

It was a question she always sort of dreaded. She loved her brother, but his story was well-known in Grosse Pointe and she got tired of being asked about it.

"He's fine," she replied evenly. "His PI business is doing

well. He's a good investigator and he stays very busy. Business is always good in Grosse Pointe."

Beau nodded.

"Okay, hopefully I'll be seeing you again soon," he said.

Ellen turned, and walked back toward where she had parked her car.

The lake looked spectacular in the late afternoon light.

It was a view, she realized, she could get used to.

CHAPTER FOUR

Coming out of unconsciousness was nothing new for Billy "Dynamite" Dawkins.

Although it had never happened to him during his professional career, he'd been knocked out many times as a youth, growing up in Detroit.

He actually laughed when he heard about NFL players suing the league for traumatic head injuries. He'd had so many traumatic brain injuries he couldn't count them, which was probably a case in point.

But now, as his eyes slowly opened, he wasn't greeted with the canvas floor of a boxing ring, or blood-splattered pavement after a street brawl.

Instead, he realized he was on a bed, staring at the ceiling.

"Looks like our little Sleeping Beauty is finally awake," a voice said off to his right.

"He knows when it's show time," another voice said.

Dawkins turned his head toward the right, and saw a man in jeans and a flannel shirt, with a beard and greasy baseball cap, leering at him. Behind him, another man, similarly dressed, but with a cowboy hat, watched him with open amusement.

"Oh, he don't look too happy," the first man said.

The man formerly known as Dynamite struggled to sit up, but couldn't move his arms. He looked down and saw he was handcuffed.

His shirt was gone and so were his socks and shoes. All he had on were his shorts, and the handcuffs.

"What the fuck?" he growled. His throat felt raw and his head hurt. He remembered the dart in his back.

He'd been tranquilized like a tiger on a nature show.

"Damn, you is a big boy, though," the guy with the cowboy hat said. "We threw you on that cot, we thought the sucker might collapse."

Dawkins realized he wasn't in a bed, like he had originally thought. It was a military-style cot. He looked around. The room was dark, with wood paneling, a wood stove in a corner, and a little kitchen. Above it, was a loft.

It was a cabin, he figured. A northwoods cabin, and he was stuck inside with two hillbillies who had apparently kidnapped him and put him in handcuffs. They'd even partially undressed him. He hoped they weren't planning to recreate any scenes from the movie Deliverance.

"You kidnapped me? You think I'm rich?" Dawkins asked.

He had put his head back down on the pillow behind him. He didn't feel like getting up just yet. He needed to think. He still felt groggy and not himself from the drugs. He wished he could have a big cup of coffee to clear his head.

"Bet this is how you used to get ready before a big fight, wasn't it?" Cowboy hat continued. Greasy Baseball Cap guy chuckled. "Wake up in the locker room, hungover from champagne and bangin' some of your groupies? Lace 'em up and get on out there and kick some ass, am I right, Dynamite?"

Dawkins actually heard the guy in the chair slap his thigh as he laughed. Like some horrible Hee Haw rerun.

"Not exactly," Dawkins said. "Who are you guys, anyway? Mind filling me in on what you've got in mind here?"

This time, he managed to sit up and swing his feet from the cot. His head swam and his vision was blurry. When they cleared, he felt a little better.

He studied the two men before him.

It was easy to see Cowboy Hat was in charge. The guy in the baseball cap must have been on guard duty. They were careful, that was clear. There was a big revolver tucked into the sitting guy's waistband. And now, Billy could see Cowboy Hat was carrying a sawed-off pump shotgun.

For the first time, he felt a little tremor of uneasiness pass through him.

This wasn't good.

They knew who he was, though.

"If you've done any kind of research, you know I'm not rich," he said. "My manager is, but I sure as hell aren't."

"You were a helluva fighter, but a bad businessman, is that right?" Cowboy Hat said.

Dawkins nodded. "Pretty good summary, I would say."

"Shit, we got a humble man here, Troy!" Cowboy Hat said.

Dawkins looked at Baseball Cap, who now had a name. "Troy, did you put these on me?" he said, holding up his cuffed hands.

"Sure did," Troy said. "What you gonna complain they're too tight? Tough shit."

Dawkins smiled at him.

"Nah, I wasn't going to complain. I was going to compliment you on a job well done. They fit perfectly.

Cowboy Hat laughed.

"Shit, this is gonna be a riot."

CHAPTER FIVE

There are several sections of I-75 North in Michigan that have always inspired a genuine emotional lift for me. Granted, I don't get out of Grosse Pointe and the Detroit area all that often, but I've occasionally escaped to the north woods of Michigan throughout my life.

It has always been a place of beautiful lakes, towering pine trees, and depending on which side of the state you visit, beautiful bluffs and awe-inspiring coastal rock formations. In fact, Michigan has more coastline than any other state in the United States.

The minivan was packed for a nice extended vacation. Isabel and Nina were in the back seats, Anna to my right, and I had my iPhone plugged into the vehicle's sound system. I'd even made a custom road trip playlist with songs involving the highway.

Right now, AC/DC's *Highway to Hell* was playing.

"John, what is this?" Anna asked, pointing at the sound system's control panel. She was frowning at me, and kind of gave a nod of the head back toward the kids. As if to say, you know, we're parents. We aren't supposed to be listening to this kind of music.

"Bon Scott and the Young brothers doing what they do best," I said. "That's what this is."

"Dad turn it off!" Isabel said. "This music is terrible."

"What are you talking about?" I said. "This is real music. Not some Justin Bieber nonsense."

I tried to compromise by turning the volume down.

"Put in Bruno Mars!" Nina said.

The highway crested a hill and as I topped it, the beauty of the state touched my often cynical and sarcastic soul. There was a valley before us, not the kind out West. This was a Midwest "valley" which really meant it was more a dip in the road, but it gave a striking panorama and the first time I felt like I was officially out of the city, and into nature.

Never mind the fact that we still had three hours to go, and Good Isle wasn't exactly "roughing" it.

"So, were you surprised when Ellen called you?" Anna asked me.

My wife was an Italian beauty, but with what her mother had warned me was a "fresh mouth." Meaning, she didn't take crap from anyone, least of all her husband.

It kept life interesting.

"Yeah, of course," I said. "I knew Ellen was having problems at work. She regularly does because there will always be a bunch of Neanderthals who don't like working for a woman. Or who feel a chief of police is a man's job."

"She knows how to handle those morons, though," Anna pointed out.

"True," I agreed. "But it has to get annoying. Dealing with that crap day in and day out."

"Does she think Good Isle will be any different?" Anna asked. "Heck, up there it might be even worse. Small towns sometimes mean small minds."

I passed a car that was going way too slow. I glanced as I

went by. A black pickup truck, jacked up, with big knobby tires, a rebel flag decal in the back window, and a bumper sticker that said 'This truck is protected by Smith & Wesson.'

"My point exactly," Anna said.

The song on my playlist changed to Bruce Springsteen's *Born To Run*. I thought this would go over better than AC/DC. I looked in my rearview mirror. Both girls had on headphones.

Sigh.

Kids these days.

"That will really suck if she likes the place and takes the job," Anna said. "It's great having her around. And Lord knows you've needed her."

I ignored the jab. At the same time, I had to admit she was right. My sister had come to my rescue many, many times. I'd helped her out occasionally, too, but we all knew the ledger was weighted to her side a lot more than mine.

"She loves helping me out," I said. "In fact, I haven't really needed her. I've just made her feel like I did because it really helps out her self-esteem. Another example of how I'm always thinking of others."

"Nice try, John," Anna said. "You didn't answer my question. What if she likes the place? What are the odds she'll take the gig?"

"A million to one," I said, bristling with confidence. "In fact, I'd bet my last dollar there's no way in hell Ellen will take this job. The town is too small. She's single. Ellen loves Detroit and all of its new, funky restaurants that are popping up all over the place."

We passed a guy on a Harley. He had on polyester pants and a short-sleeved dress shirt. One of those middle-aged rebel accountants. I felt like telling him the twenty grand he spent on the bike probably wasn't going to help him with the ladies.

"I'm sure she could find places to go and things to do up here," Anna said, ever the optimist. That endless positivity was something I'd had to overcome in my marriage. Most of the time it just really bugged me.

"Up here?" I continued. "Yeah, there's a few good places, but that's it. And I don't think there are a lot of romantic options."

"Hmm, I'm not so sure about that," Anna said. "My friend, Colleen, moved to Traverse City, met a freelance movie producer and they fell in love and got married in like six months. They go to Los Angeles all the time, especially during winter. She couldn't be happier."

Hmm, Anna sounded wistful. I thought about mentioning that, and then thought better of it.

"You sound wistful," I said, ignoring my own advice, like always.

Anna rolled her eyes.

We drove on, deeper into the north woods as traffic thinned out and we saw more and more pickup trucks, wide farm fields full of potatoes, corn and soybeans, and the occasional picturesque red farmhouse. The kind that was becoming more and more rare these days.

Eventually, we turned off the freeway and made our way west, and the road rose before us, getting steeper and more dramatic as we neared the shore of Lake Michigan.

And then finally, one last rise and the beautiful blue of the Great Lake was before us.

"Wow," Anna said. She turned and told the girls to take off their headphones.

"Lovely," I said.

"If I were Ellen, and they offered me the job," Anna said, "I'd take it in a heartbeat."

CHAPTER SIX

"Welcome to the Northwoods Lodge," the cute young woman in khakis and a blue short-sleeved polo shirt said to us. Her name tag indicated her name was Crystal.

"Hi," I said as I stepped out of the minivan. It had only been a four-hour drive but I felt stiff and I stifled a yawn. The fresh air was refreshing.

The girls piled out. "Where's the pool?" Isabel asked.

"It's right behind the main lobby," Crystal said. "Let's get you checked in so you can jump right in." She smiled and I guessed she was either a college student or a recent grad, maybe earning some extra cash before grad school.

I loaded our suitcases onto a cart, amazed at how many there were.

"You do realize we're here for four days, not four weeks," I said to Anna.

"We have to have options, John," she replied.

We entered the lobby and it was all exposed pine, rustic bronze hardware and dark brown leather. A giant stuffed moose occupied one corner. A towering fireplace was on one side of the lobby and the girls naturally headed straight for the bank of windows that overlooked the giant pool and water slide.

There was even a lazy river, with kids and adults alike floating around, some of the grown-ups sporting big fruity drinks.

Ellen had texted me and told me to use her name at check-in, which I did. And soon, we were opening the door to a very large suite. It was all rustic furniture, just like the lobby, and featured a balcony that overlooked rolling hills covered in evergreen trees.

The girls took one bedroom and Anna and I the other.

We were unpacking and getting settled when there was a knock on the door.

"Aunt Ellen!" the girls called out. They ran to her as she entered the room and I had to smile. I was so used to seeing her in her police uniform with her gun belt, it sort of caught me off guard to see her in jeans, a pair of running shoes, and a vintage Rolling Stones t-shirt.

"You look like you've moved up here already," I said.

"When in Rome," she replied. She hugged the girls and Anna.

"I've got to get these girls into the pool," Anna said. "Are you going to join us?" she asked Ellen.

"I wouldn't miss it for the world," Ellen said. She turned to me. "Please don't wear your thong, though. There are kids down there."

"How about my European Speedo?" I asked.

"How about not?"

With incredible foresight, I had also stocked various alcoholic beverages including beer and wine. So, when I arrived on the pool deck, I found Ellen sitting at a table watching the girls play, and Anna was swimming laps.

I twisted the tops off of two beers and handed one to Ellen.

"Here's to Good Isle," I said.

"To Good Isle," Ellen replied, and we clinked bottles.

"Well?" I asked.

She shrugged her shoulders. "It's nice. A beautiful place. Very different."

"A bad kind of different or a good kind of different?"

"I'm not really sure yet. It could be boring."

"What's that line Brian Dennehy's character said in First Blood? Something like 'You might even say this town is boring. But we like it that way.'"

"Leave it to you to quote First Blood in a job discussion."

"Hey, there's a lot of wisdom in that movie," I said. "Like you can bring down a police chopper with a big rock if you throw it just right."

Ellen took a drink of her beer.

"So what's the timeline?" I persisted. "When are you going to find out what they think?"

"Supposedly there's a meeting tomorrow to discuss the final candidates," she said, smiling at the girls in the pool who were doing some kind of bizarre water ballet moves. "I was the last interview, I guess. I don't know how many others they're considering."

"What's your gut tell you?" I asked.

"No idea. There's always the woman thing," she said, her voice tired.

"Yeah."

The girls were having a blast and Anna was powering through her swimming strokes. The woman could really swim. I was a terrible swimmer. The doggy paddle was my default swimming style.

"If you move up here, you won't be able to help me out on my cases," I pointed out.

She looked at me out of the corner of her eye. "And your point would be...?"

I laughed. "Point taken. But still, wouldn't it be weird to leave Grosse Pointe?"

"It's only four hours away. Plus, you and Anna and the girls would have a place to visit."

I looked at her. "You sound like you're seriously considering it. I told Anna there'd be no way in hell you'd come up here. You're too much of a city girl."

"Who the hell knows?"

Her phone buzzed and she looked down at it.

"Hmm. It's Beau Gordon. You remember him?" she asked me. "He's the one who recommended me for the job."

"Sure, I remember him," I said.

Ellen stood up and walked away as she answered the phone. There was a table nearby and I guessed she preferred talking to Beau in private.

The beer tasted really sweet, and I was debating about joining my family in the pool. I saw on one end there was a diving board and I knew how much my girls loved my famous John Rockne belly flop. They howled every time I performed it, which was pretty much every time I was in a swimming pool.

Suddenly, a shadow fell over me and I glanced up to see Ellen standing behind me. She had her cell phone in her hand, extended toward me.

"What?" I asked. "I thought you were talking to Beau Gordon."

"I was," she replied. "But he wants to talk to you.

CHAPTER SEVEN

"What?"

Anna stood before me, dripping wet, her hair plastered back over her head like a skull cap. The girls were still swimming in the pool, I could hear their shrieks and yelps as they took turns tipping one another over from their floaty rings.

"I have a meeting," I said.

Ellen and Anna both stood looking at me.

"What do you mean, a meeting?" Anna asked me. "You don't know a soul up here."

"Do you remember Beau Gordon?" I asked. "From Grosse Pointe?"

"Yeah, what about him?"

"He just called. He's the guy who recommended Ellen for the job up here."

"What does he want with you?" Anna asked.

I could see why she was a little miffed. It was supposed to be a weekend family getaway and here I was mixing business with pleasure, about to leave her alone with the kids.

"I don't know," I said, honestly. "He said he knew Ellen

was having us up here, and that something came up he needs to discuss with me immediately. It sounds like maybe a case."

"You can't work a case up here," Anna said. "You don't live here."

Ellen walked away from us, not wanting to get into the middle of any marital situation. I wished I could've done the same.

I glanced over to make sure Ellen was out of earshot range. She was.

"Look, if this guy is friends with the city council, and Ellen is interested in the job, I would have to be a real asshole to blow this guy off. What if he called up the city council and said he changed his mind about Ellen? Because her brother is such a dick that he wasn't willing to drive across a small town to meet with him?"

Anna worked her towel vigorously, wiping down her long, lean legs. She looked incredibly sexy.

She caught me looking at her.

"Focus, John," she said, narrowing her eyes at me.

"Okay, look," I said. "He's five minutes away. I'll pop over there, it probably won't take more than an hour, and then I'll be right back. You know, I am a businessman and maybe there's some money here."

It was an obvious ploy, but also the truth.

"Take some chewing gum," she said, instantly becoming practical once the decision had been made. "Showing up with beer breath probably isn't the smartest idea."

I gave her a quick kiss, tasted the chlorine from the pool and then Ellen and I went out to the minivan. Beau had invited her as well.

"What do you think this is all about?" I asked. "Do you think he's inviting us over to tell you that you got the job?"

Ellen shook her head. "No, the meeting where they're deciding on who to offer the job is tomorrow, supposedly.

And I highly doubt he would have invited you if that's why he called. No, this is about something else."

I plugged the address Beau had given me into my phone and used the navigation app to show me the route to his house.

We left the resort area, turned left from the main street of Good Isle, and drove down to a narrow two-way road that hugged the shore of the lake. The houses here were monsters, every bit as big and grand as the mansions in Grosse Pointe along Lake Shore Road.

They were different, though.

Instead of a lot of dark brick and Tudor-style homes, these all had a beach feel, albeit on an extremely luxurious scale. There was a lot of painted white trim, cedar shake, and wide, expansive porches with bench swings. I knew from past trips these houses went for millions upon millions of dollars.

Partly because the area was a beacon for three sets of people with money.

You had the wealthy folks from the Greater Detroit area, who shot straight up I-75 and could be in their beachfront mansion within four hours, less if you drove above the speed limit, which most of them did.

The next group was from Chicago. They could head east out of the city, hug the bottom of Lake Michigan, and make their way up along the coast in a little over five hours. In fact, communities along that whole stretch of western Michigan had summer residents from Chicago.

And lastly, the smallest group was from the small city of Grand Rapids, for whom the trip was very short.

"I thought you said you wanted a change from Grosse Pointe," I said to Ellen.

"The difference is Grosse Pointe is between a lake and Detroit. Good Isle is between a lake and a bunch of corn fields."

She had me there.

We finally pulled up into one of the biggest and grandest homes along this stretch of Good Isle's shores.

It was cedar shake painted beige, with white trim and two towering chimneys made with natural rock that bookended the property. We entered from the rear of the estate, but could see out past the structure to the lake. Which meant they had a huge stretch of beachfront property.

I let out a low whistle.

"Beau has done mighty well for himself."

We parked next to a Mercedes G-Wagon and walked to the back porch, which was huge and looked like you could dine on its immaculate wooden boards. Everything in Good Isle was just so damned *clean*.

I rang the doorbell and looked down. I realized I was still wearing my swimming suit. Ellen caught me glancing at myself.

"Nice attire," she said. "Did you think we were going to meet in the lake?"

The door opened, saving me from a quick-witted reply that I didn't have, and a matronly woman looked out at us.

"Hi, I'm here to meet with Beau. John Rockne. This is my sister, Ellen."

She smiled, greeted us warmly and welcomed us inside.

It was a spectacular space with a towering center hall, huge wooden doors on each side, and a grand staircase that wound its way upstairs.

We followed the woman to the door on the left. She cracked it open, said something quietly, and then opened the door for us.

With a gesture, I let Ellen go in first.

We stepped into a huge library and the door thudded shut behind us.

8.

"There they are!" Beau Gordon stood up from a brown leather couch that was in front of a huge fireplace. There were leather club chairs on each side of the couch, and in one of them was a petite blonde woman with small, dark eyes. She too, stood.

"Hi Beau," Ellen said. She crossed to him and I followed.

"Ellen, good to see you again," Beau said. They hugged, and I stuck out my hand.

"John, good to see you, too," he said. Beau was a little older than I remembered him, a little heavier, but overall still the same. He looked exactly like what he was, a retired high-powered Grosse Pointe attorney who had done very well and was used to the status and prestige he'd earned over the years.

"Let me introduce you to Lindsey Nordegren," Beau said. The woman shook hands with us and I noticed how slight her build was. Her hand was small, and her bones seemed very delicate. But I also sensed an intensity in her dark eyes and there had been no shortage of strength in her grip.

"Lindsey is my wife's youngest sister," Beau explained. "Can I get you something to drink?" He gestured toward a serving table off to the side that held a decanter, probably filled with cognac or expensive scotch, as well as a carafe that most likely contained coffee.

"No, thank you," I said.

"I'm fine, but thank you," Ellen added.

"Okay then, please, have a seat, I'd like to discuss a matter with you."

Beau went back to his spot on the couch, and Lindsey eased back into the club chair. Ellen took the other club chair and I joined Beau on the couch.

The room was impressive. There were floor-to-ceiling

bookshelves on each side, filled with law books but I also saw some literary classics as well as popular non-fiction. The wall behind Beau's massive wooden desk held framed law degrees and photos of Beau with mostly Detroit-area celebrities.

"This is a highly confidential discussion so I hope you will treat it as such," Beau stated, in his most lawyerly voice.

"Of course," I replied.

He glanced over at Lindsey.

"Linds, why don't I start, and then I'll turn it over to you?" he asked.

"That's fine," she answered.

"My sister-in-law, as you can see, is a very beautiful woman. She's also kind, funny and very intelligent. She's also married. To a well-known financier who makes Good Isle his part-time home. Lindsey is committed to the marriage, which is why we wanted to discuss this matter in private."

I noticed that Beau had said Lindsey was committed to the marriage, as opposed to saying she was in love and committed to her husband. Big difference.

Beau turned to Lindsey and inclined his head to indicate that it was now time for her to take over.

She cleared her throat.

"Yes, I am committed to my marriage. However, I'm often here, in Good Isle, alone. My husband travels constantly and sometimes I get very lonely."

Suddenly, I realized where this was going.

"I met a man who also has a place here, part-time. We became...involved."

Beau shifted in his seat and I realized the conversation had just crossed some kind of invisible line of comfort for him.

"That man has now disappeared," Lindsay said. "And I don't think he went voluntarily."

She took a deep breath and Beau was about step in, but she beat him to it.

"I want you to find him," she said, her voice firm. "I can't go to the police because of the sensitivity of the issue and this is a small town."

There was a pause and I was about to ask my first question but Beau cut me off.

"Lindsey came to me, not knowing what to do," he explained. He turned to Ellen. "And you and I had just met for coffee, during which you'd mentioned John was arriving today."

Ellen nodded.

"And since I know John is a private investigator, it seemed serendipitous."

Another pause, and this time I knew my questions were welcome.

"I guess the first question I have is how do you know your friend didn't leave Good Isle of his own volition?" I asked.

Lindsey took another deep breath.

"Several things," she said. "Number one, we were supposed to meet last night, and he's extremely good about communication. It seems he was raised to be punctual, almost to a fault." Her face broke into a smile and everything about her changed. Suddenly, she looked extremely beautiful, charismatic even.

I came to the sudden and definite conclusion that her husband was a dunderheaded fool to leave her alone all the time.

"So, you didn't hear from him?" Ellen asked.

"No. Not a phone call. A text. Nothing."

"What else?"

Lindsey rubbed her tiny, pale hands on her thighs. "I have a key to his place and I went over there this morning after I hadn't heard from him. He had taken some chicken out of the freezer to thaw for dinner tonight. He had some shirts that I know he was planning to drop off today. In short, nothing looked like a man who was about to take off."

It didn't add up for me. Maybe he'd zipped down to Detroit for something and was planning on being back this afternoon. It seemed way too early to panic.

"Is there something else?" I asked. "A reason for the sense of urgency?"

"Yes," Lindsey answered. "He drives an old Ford Bronco SUV. Silver. It's one of his prized possessions. It's vintage and he babies it like it's a human being."

She turned her head and looked into the fireplace.

"He loves to fish and he always fishes in the same spot, and parks in the same place near the pier," she said. "A friend of mine saw his Bronco driving away from the pier yesterday, but he wasn't driving. Someone else was."

I waited for the other shoe to drop.

"The driver was a hillbilly-looking guy," Lindsay said. "Greasy baseball cap. Beard. There's just no way in hell he should have been driving that car."

"Maybe it was a mechanic," Ellen said.

"Or someone taking it for a test drive. Maybe your friend was selling it."

"No way anyone else would touch that Bronco," Lindsay said, adamant. "No way on God's green Earth."

"Did your friend have any enemies? Do you know of someone who would have wanted to do him harm?" Ellen asked.

We all knew the answer to that.

The husband, that's who.

If he knew about the affair, that was. Which it definitely sounded like he didn't.

But Lindsey surprised us.

"He had a lot of enemies," she said. "That's just the thing."

Finally, I got to the point.

"I guess the question needs to be asked. Who is your friend?"

Lindsey closed her eyes.

"Billy Dawkins."

I felt my breath catch in my throat.

"Dynamite Dawkins?" I said, my voice almost a whisper.

"Yes," Lindsey said.

CHAPTER EIGHT

At least they hadn't knocked him out this time.

He was guessing, but Dawkins assumed they didn't want the hassle of trying to haul his carcass to their vehicle, which was probably a junky-ass pickup truck. That would be too much work. These two shitheads would take the easy way out every time.

Of that, he was sure.

Dawkins wasn't surprised when they put a gun in his ribs and told him to walk out to the truck. A lot less work for them and he didn't mind. They could've stuck a needle in his shoulder but he had always hated drugs. Booze had been a different story, but powder and pills were never his thing.

Plus, he'd learned over the years that it was always better to be conscious than unconscious. That way, you at least knew what was happening, even if you didn't like it.

"Let's go, boy," the man with the cowboy hat said.

Dawkins walked forward, out of the cabin.

"What's your name?" he asked. He got tired of thinking of him as the man in the cowboy hat.

"Let's go with Boss," the man said. "Yeah, I like that. Why don't you call me Boss?"

Troy snickered softly behind him, and jabbed the muzzle of the gun deeper into Dawkins's ribs.

He didn't move, or answer.

The man in the cowboy hat laughed. "You don't like that much, do you?"

"Well I was just gonna call you Pecker Head," Dawkins said. "I actually think that fits you better."

An easy smile crossed Dawkins's face after he delivered the insult. He looked around and there was absolutely nothing he could see other than trees. Nothing but pines and two pickup trucks.

Finally, his gaze settled back on the guy in the cowboy hat who clearly hadn't liked being called a pecker head.

Well tough shit, Dawkins thought.

"What did you two geniuses do with my Bronco?" he asked.

He felt himself starting to get pissed off. They had fucked with him, and for that they would pay, and pay dearly. But nobody fucked with his Bronco.

"Oh, it's in a safe place," Boss said. "Don't you worry your big ugly head over it."

Dawkins looked over and saw a garage with fresh tire tracks in the dirt path leading up to it. That's where his Bronco was, he was sure of it. That's why these two hillbillies—

Lights exploded along his eyes and his head snapped to the left as something crashed into his jaw. He stayed on his feet, and his head instantly cleared. He crouched, ready to fight, but then remembered his hands were still cuffed.

He looked back at Boss who was standing there grinning and shaking his fist. "Boy, you sure can take a punch," he said.

Dawkins's eyes narrowed. He could take a punch, that was certain. He'd always been known for his iron jaw.

"Careful there, Darnell," Troy said. "This boy's a mean sumbitch."

The man formerly known as Boss rolled his eyes. "Troy, you dumb shit, you just told him my name," he said.

"It don't matter," Troy said.

Dawkins wondered what exactly he meant by that.

Darnell and Troy.

Two fucking redneck hillbillies, he thought to himself

Troy jammed the rifle into Dawkins's side and forced his way forward to the pickup truck that was second in line in the driveway. They opened the upper door of the camper top and then opened the tailgate.

Darnell reached into the bed of the truck and pulled out a chain.

"Hold your hands out in front of you, Dynamite," he said, his voice full of sarcasm. "Bet they don't call you that anymore. Your fuse done run out a long time ago."

Troy giggled behind them.

Dawkins did as instructed and Darnell locked the chain onto the handcuffs.

"Now get in," Darnell said.

Dawkins climbed over the tailgate and slid along the floor of the truck into the back. Behind him, his captors hoisted the tailgate back up and put the camper's hinged door down. Something clicked and Dawkins knew he was locked inside.

He looked around.

The back of the truck was filthy and smelled like shit. Even in the dim light he could make out some ropes, a bag of fertilizer and some greasy rags.

Two door slammed up front and then he heard the engine fire up. He felt the truck being backed out and soon they were going down one of those washboard country roads and

Dawkins felt sure some of the fillings in his teeth were going to rattle out.

Up front there was country music and then Dawkins could smell marijuana.

As they bounced down shitty country roads, he thought about what he might be in for.

Someone had ordered his kidnapping, of that he was sure.

He had a few theories of who it might've been; after all, he had a lot of enemies not just Good Isle, Michigan but also in Detroit and frankly, all across the country. During his career, he'd pissed off a lot of people.

There was no way these two jokers were working for themselves. They didn't have enough IQ between them to light a campfire. Although, Darnell seemed to have some animal cunning. Troy was a walking tree stump.

The drive took nearly two hours and by the end of it Dawkins still had zero answers.

But when the truck stopped, one of his theories was proven true because just before they opened the door to the rear of the truck he heard a sound that was very familiar to him.

His fists clenched instinctively.

There was no mistaking the sound as he'd heard it dozens and dozens of times throughout his career.

It was unmistakable.

It was the sound of a crowd cheering.

CHAPTER NINE

Beau was paying, everyone decided. It would just be easier that way. Lindsey's husband was extremely fastidious with the household's finances, even if he didn't pay a whole lot of attention to his wife.

"He's got a real passion for our checkbook," Lindsey had explained.

Ellen was once again surprised at how life was a nonstop cavalcade of unforeseen incidents. You woke up in the morning and figured where you'd be at by the end of the day, and quite often, it turned out you were wrong.

It's what made life both interesting and an occasional pain in the ass.

Like today, for instance. She had imagined she would spend the day hanging out by the pool with her brother and his family, and instead, she was a co-investigator into the disappearance of a legendary Detroit boxer named Billy "Dynamite" Dawkins.

It would have to be handled carefully.

"John, my involvement in this will have to be handled delicately," she said. "And let's be honest, discretion isn't your strong suit."

"I know," he replied. "I think this might be the first time I've ever heard you and the word 'delicate' in the same sentence."

"Good Isle may not have a chief of police right now, but they still have a police force," Ellen said. "And it wouldn't look good if one of their job candidates started poking around in an active investigation. Especially as I'm still the chief of police in Grosse Pointe."

"Don't worry, delicate flower," John answered. "I'll handle the investigation. You can hang out with Anna and the girls. Be a surrogate parent."

"Right," Ellen said. "I'll follow your lead. Let the girls do whatever they want, make sure I follow Anna's orders, and try not to make a mess."

"That about sums it up. You'll have to cut the grass, too."

Ellen laughed. She actually thought her brother was a great dad, but she would never admit that or tell him. The Rockne family was more into dry humor, than outright, open affection.

It made it more fun, if not always as warm and mushy as other families.

"Have you got a plan?" Ellen asked. "Or are you going to wing it like you usually do?"

Out of the corner of her eye, she saw John look out the window. He always did that while he was thinking. He rarely answered instantly, preferring to think through what he was going to say.

"First, I plan to go to the site of his disappearance," he said. "Someone may have seen something, in addition to Lindsey's friend. A marina can be a busy place. Maybe some of the other fishermen saw something."

That's what Ellen would have done.

"What about his place?" she asked.

Lindsey had given John her key to Dynamite's house. She had told them it was a historic house in the downtown section of Good Isle, that the retired boxer had totally renovated. Ellen got the impression that Dynamite liked old, vintage things. His Bronco. And his house. He sounded like an interesting man.

"I'll go there after the fishing pier," John said. "Unless..."

"Unless what?"

"Unless you get tired of hanging out with the Rockne clan and want to check out Dawkins's house," he said, with that expression on his face he always got when he was asking her to do him a favor. It wasn't terribly subtle. "A historic house?" he continued. "That sounds like it's right up your alley."

Ellen's house in Grosse Pointe was a labor of love for her. And the thought of leaving that house was almost impossible to imagine. She'd restored every inch of it. But then again, it had been done for several years now.

Maybe she was ready for a new project.

She could make a lot of money from that house downstate, and the cash would go a long way up here. Despite the enormous price tags of lakefront homes, quite a few houses downtown in the historic district were probably very affordable and ripe for renovation.

"Let me sleep on that little tidbit," she finally said to John.

They got back to the resort, and while John went back to his room and to his family, Ellen returned to her room.

She put her keys and purse on the desk by the bed and reached into her little refrigerator. She, too, had stocked up on some alcoholic beverages and she pulled out a beer, twisted off the cap and went out to her little balcony.

Ellen had grabbed her iPad as well and as she took the first few sips of beer, she looked out at the trees. Her view was amazing in that to the left, she could see Lake Michigan.

And right now, the sun had faded but the sky was a brilliant orange with undertones of red and pink.

"Beautiful," she said to herself.

After several minutes of quiet contemplation, she launched the email on her iPad and read through everything. Nothing important, and she made a few cursory responses and then closed her email.

She launched the browser, and spent nearly a half hour reading about the life and times of Billy "Dynamite" Dawkins. A young, tough kid who grew up on the mean streets of Detroit. Apparently, his parents were nowhere to be found and an owner of a boxing gym had rescued him from the streets.

Before long, the skinny white kid was knocking out men twice his age. Soon, there were rumors that he might be the next great boxer to come out of the Motor City.

As his reputation grew, so did the caliber of his opponents. But Kid Dynamite, as he was called when he was still very young, knocked them all out.

And then a scandal hit.

Rumors of organized crime's involvement with Dynamite's manager and promoter were leaked to the press. An investigation ensued and Billy Dawkins lost his next match, the first loss of his career.

People lost a lot of money on that fight, and some claimed he had thrown it, but Dawkins never spoke to anyone.

He came back with a vengeance, though, and knocked out his next twelve opponents. He was one fight away from a shot at the title when disaster struck.

A detached retina.

The very same injury that had paused the career of the great Sugar Ray Leonard.

Doctors had told him not to fight, that he would go blind with one wrong punch.

So he retired.

He had the operation, but it was botched.

And he had to have it again.

By then, he was past his prime and he never fought professionally again.

Ellen snapped her iPad shut and got herself another beer.

One fight away from a shot at the title.

That must have sucked, royally.

She lifted her beer toward the distant lake.

"Dynamite, I hope I find you and get to meet you. You sound like a helluva guy."

CHAPTER TEN

For me, it's all about compromise. Marriage, that is. And when I say compromise, I mean it's all about my wife making the necessary compromises.

Kidding, of course.

But Anna is a reasonable woman and when I told her about the meeting with Beau Gordon and the actual check I'd been handed, she became a lot more understanding. So as soon as the girls were up, I took them to a nearby nature trail and we had a nice walk, some goofing around and then we stopped for donuts and coffee. No coffee for the kids. Anna would kill me.

Once we were back at the resort, we did the switch-off. Anna got the kids and I immediately took the minivan and drove down to the fishing pier.

It was easy to spot, because it was one of the key points of Good Isle's downtown. It had only one marina, and one giant pier that thrust its way out into Lake Michigan.

A fishing boat was just pulling out of the harbor, out to troll for some salmon and lake trout. Its steady drone from the engine was the only sound, except for the occasional squawk of a seagull looking for breakfast.

The town had been sleepy as I drove though it, people just finishing their late breakfasts and figuring out what they were going to be doing for the day.

I couldn't stop imagining Ellen here, working as chief of police. Would she love it initially because it was so calm and peaceful and quiet? And then a few months later would she find herself being driven batshit crazy by the lack of any, you know...crime?

Well, who really knew? And how could anyone predict what it would be like? It seemed like one of those things that would only become known once you made the leap.

Plus, I caught the logic flaw in my thinking.

Here I was talking about a lack of crime, and I was on my way to a missing persons investigation. I figured it wouldn't be much, though. A retired boxer, missing after fishing from the local pier?

He'd either fallen in the lake and been carried to the bottom or out into deeper water. Boxers had a ton of brain injuries for obvious reasons. Maybe he'd had an aneurism or a stroke and toppled off the pier into the lake. It was possible.

Or, it was quite possible he'd gone back to Detroit, ditching his married girlfriend in the process. Professional athletes were well-known for their success with the ladies. Maybe he had multiple girlfriends in multiple cities and was just making the rounds. Like a rock band with a summer of tour dates.

Even cynicism felt out of place in Good Isle.

I found my way to the pier, parked, and walked out onto the wooden dock. It was impressive. Very long, and the size of the boats parked nearby was impressive. There were some monster yachts that probably cost eight figures.

The lake was eerily calm, like a sheet of blue-green glass.

No one was on the beach as it was still very cool, and a few lonely fishermen on the pier stood guarding their fishing poles. But nothing was moving.

I made my way to each fisherman, casually chatting them up about what was biting or not, and asking if they'd seen Billy Dawkins. None of them had, but they all knew who he was, that he fished on the same pier frequently and inquired after him.

Keeping in mind the need for discretion, I just claimed to be an old friend from Detroit looking for him.

One guy suggested I talk to Herb in the marina office.

I left the pier, nosed around until I located the marina office and found a young woman, similar to the one who worked at the resort. She was young, perky and I guessed that her name wasn't Herb.

The office looked like it belonged to an old man. There was a famous Farrah Fawcett poster from forty some years ago tacked to the wall, stained coffee cups, and the unmistakable scent of an old guy.

"Are you Herb?" I asked.

She laughed. "No. Tonya. Herb called in sick today. I normally work in the restaurant, but they told me to come down here and act like I know what I'm doing."

She was cute as a button, this Tonya. Smart, articulate, and, I hoped gullible.

"Oh, I was supposed to drop off a check for Herb from his old employer down in Detroit. Do you know his home address?"

"Ah, sure," she said. She looked at a piece of paper tacked to the bulletin board. She ran her finger down a list of what I guessed was employees and their contact information.

"Let's see," she said. "Herb Watters. Ah, here it is. 729 Maple Avenue."

"Great, thank you," I said. "By the way, I love what you've done with the place."

Tonya grimaced. "Yeah, I guess I should spray some deodorizer around this place or something."

"That would probably piss off Herb. Old guys hate change."

Back in the parking lot, I studied the vehicles next to the fishing pier. I wondered where Dynamite's favorite parking space was.

I figured if he drove a vintage Bronco that was his pride and joy, he would have parked in the safest spot imaginable. There was a corner parking space, bordered by trees on one side, the farthest spot from the pier and the marina.

It was currently empty.

I walked over to it and studied the ground.

There was a stray piece of fishing line, an oil stain, and some loose gravel.

Nothing else.

I went back to the minivan, fired it up, and plugged 729 Maple Avenue into my navigation app. It took me less than five minutes to pull up in front of a tiny white house, with a white picket fence, and a twenty-year-old Chevy pickup in the driveway.

If there was ever a house that looked like it was owned by an old, single man, this would be it. I was just guessing that Herb was single. Maybe I was wrong. But there was no garage and only one car.

Or was his wife at work?

For some reason, I didn't think so.

I parked on the street, got out and looked up and down the neighborhood. It was an older section of town, clearly, but not a prosperous one. The houses all looked like they'd been slapped together quickly in the fifties or sixties and no one had bothered to do any additions or renovations. No fancy cars on the street, either. Mostly trucks and older sedans. A lot of Buicks and Fords.

They like to buy American up north.

I rang the doorbell but there was no answer.

That truck in the driveway was Herb's as sure as I knew my pants were on correctly. Which meant he was home. Unless he was, in fact, married and the little lady had carted him off somewhere.

Another press of the doorbell caused some commotion inside and the door was pulled back just slightly.

The stench of liquor wafted into my nostrils.

"Herb?"

"What do you want?" he asked.

I could just make out a gray face, bloodshot eyes and a wrinkled shirt.

"I want to ask you about Billy Dawkins," I said. "I'm a private investigator."

There was an audible gasp behind the door.

"Oh no," he said.

CHAPTER ELEVEN

"You got some ID?" he asked me. "You don't look like you're from around here, but I better be safe than sorry. Lot of crazies out there."

I showed him my driver's license and a PI card the good state of Michigan had provided me.

"Hmph," he said.

Finally, the door opened and I stepped into a cloud of gin vapors.

My first thought was, *who drinks gin anymore?*

While the house looked vaguely cute from the outside, the inside was a different story. Apparently, Herb didn't know how to use a vacuum or a mop and apparently there were no cleaning services in Good Isle because Herb's house was a pig sty.

There was a living room set made out of corduroy cloth and plywood, a sagging entertainment center with a television that had to be twenty years old, and a card table that served as the dining room table.

On the card table was a big glass of orange juice.

No doubt laced with bargain-basement gin.

"I can't help you," he said. "I don't even know why I let you in."

"I have a very trusting face," I said.

Herb looked at me, trying to gauge if I was correct.

"How about I ask you a couple of questions before we make that determination," I said. I wished I could plug my nose because it smelled bad. Asking him to crack a window would be terribly bad manners.

"Wanna crack a window?" I asked.

"Go ahead and ask your questions," he said. "I've got a doctor's appointment in a half hour," he said.

It was as if he just remembered he was supposed to be sick. A doctor's appointment. Yeah, right. With Dr. Cheap Gin.

"Billy Dawkins," I said. "Also known as Dynamite. Have you seen him lately?"

Herb shook his head back and forth so energetically he looked like a dog who'd just gotten out of a swimming pool and was trying to dry its fur.

"Nope. Nada."

He took a big drink of his orange juice. I wondered if Herb was as bad a liar when he was sober. Because he was terrible at it when he was drunk. Which is what he was now.

"Do you know him?" I asked.

"Sure, of course," he said. His tired, old face seemed to light up. "Everyone knows Dynamite. The man's a legend! One of the girls at the office used the computer to find video of his old fights and we all watched a greatest hits movie. Get it? Greatest hits!"

Herb made a punching motion, like a left cross, and sloshed some of his gin and juice mixture onto the carpet. He didn't notice.

"Those were some exciting fights," I said. I'd watched a few of them myself on YouTube.

"That man was a beast," Herb said.

I hoped he used the past tense because he was talking about Dynamite's fighting career, and not because of something more sinister.

"And he lives here now!" Herb said. "Right here in Good Isle! Year round!"

It seemed almost a shame to ruin Herb's obvious man-crush, but I had to ask. "Know anyone who would want to harm him?"

Herb's face went slack. He was absolutely plastered and I wondered if this was an everyday activity, or if something else was going on.

"Not here in this town, no way. He's like a local treasure."

"Did you see anything two days ago? He was last seen fishing from the pier."

"Nope."

It was bullshit. Herb was lying and I had no idea why.

"Why are you lying?"

He nearly spit out his juice. Instead, it was like some kind of wet spluttering sound.

"The hell did you just say?" he asked.

In all of the years of interrogation, I'd pissed off plenty of people. But this old, drunk guy wasn't going to be any kind of match. I could push him and he would topple over.

"I just don't think you're being honest, Herb. I also don't think you're sick. So why didn't you want to go to work today? Did something happen at the pier? Something at the marina involving Billy Dawkins that you don't want anything to do with?"

I had pretty much nailed it because Herb looked like a balloon in a rapid state of deflation.

He kind of staggered to his feet. I could see the indecision in his face. Tell me the truth, or tell me to get the hell out of his house.

"Get the hell out of my house," he said.

"The truth is going to come out eventually, Herb," I said. "It's really for the best if you tell me what you saw and what you know. Believe me, if any harm has come to Dynamite Dawkins, you'll want to be on the side of the good guys."

I idly wondered if Herb had a gun. Maybe a deer rifle of some sort he could stagger down the hallway and retrieve, come back and try to shoot me.

Something told me his aim wouldn't be very impressive.

"What the goddamned heck do you mean the side of the good guys?" he slobbered at me. "I am a good guy!"

He was bellowing now, like a drunk in a bar at two a.m., pissed off the bartender was closing up shop.

"Prove it, then," I said. "Tell me what you saw."

Suddenly, Herb's face caved in and I thought the man might start crying.

But he didn't.

He started spilling.

"Okay, look," he said. "I never saw Dynamite. My boss told me to stay away from him."

"Why?"

Herb got up, made no pretense of what he was doing, went into the kitchen and returned with a gin bottle. He poured it into his juice glass.

"You're going to kill yourself if you drink that much," I said. "Why don't you have a glass of water instead?"

Herb ignored me.

"I used to bug Billy when he was fishing," Herb said. "He never complained, in fact, I think he kinda liked me. But it would piss my boss off when he saw me out on the pier yakking with Billy when I was supposed to be in the marina office. But do you know how boring that can get?"

He took a drink of his juice.

"Jesus Chee-rist! Nothing happens there some days. Can you blame me?"

I shook my head.

"Anyway, Wednesday, I saw Billy leaving the pier after he was done fishing," Herb said. "Or at least, I saw his Ford Bronco leaving."

Herb looked out of the corner of his eye at the living room. As if someone was sneaking up to steal his 1970s recliner.

"Only Billy wasn't driving," he added.

"Who was?"

"I don't know," Herb said again. But his voice had changed. It was his dishonest mode.

"Yes you do," I said.

"I don't know!" he said, shouting at me. "It was a guy, that's all I know. With a ball cap pulled down way over his face. But it wasn't Billy! Now get the hell out of my house before I call the cops."

Since I already felt half-drunk from the fumes, I decided to cut my losses. Or cut bait, as they say up north.

I gave Herb one of my business cards.

"When you're done with your orange juice binge, and remember more of the truth, give me a call."

Herb waved me away and I went to the front door.

"Yeah, yeah, yeah," he said. "Get out of here."

CHAPTER TWELVE

"How is the parent thing going?" I asked Ellen on the phone.

"I'm doing exactly what you do: watching Anna take care of everyone and everything," Ellen answered. "She's quite good at this. You should have her give you some pointers."

"It's a tough gig, isn't it?"

"I don't know how you do it."

"Listen," I said. "I just got done chatting with an old guy who works in the marina office. You and he have the exact same living room furniture set, by the way."

"I can only imagine," Ellen said.

"Anyway, he claims he saw someone else driving Dynamite's Bronco away from the fishing pier."

"We already knew that. Lindsey's secret friend told her that. A guy in a greasy baseball cap and a beard, right?"

"My old drunk friend confirmed the baseball cap but he didn't mention the beard. Still, I think he and Lindsey's source saw the same guy."

"Maybe the old guy is Lindsey's witness."

"I don't think so," I said, trying to imagine beautiful Lindsey Nordegren in Herb Watters's house.

"Probably doesn't matter," Ellen said. "Still, it would be nice if Lindsey told us who her witness was."

"Lotta secrets in this little town," I pointed out.

"Everyone's got 'em."

"So how do you feel about going to check out Billy Dawkins's house with me? Can you break away from your foster parenting gig?"

"Again, I'll emulate you and ask Anna for permission to leave the house," Ellen said.

Boy, she could sure get snarky.

There was a pause and then Ellen came back on the line.

"Swing by the resort's parking lot and pick me up. Anna gave me the okay."

One nice thing about Good Isle was its size. Driving "across town" took about five minutes.

I pulled up to the entrance of the resort and Ellen hopped in.

"You look like a real badass private investigator in your minivan," she observed. "I'm sure it strikes fear into the hearts of bad guys everywhere."

"It seats seven bad guys comfortably," I said. "For the long drive to the big house."

She sighed and looked out the window.

"Today's the day of the committee meeting," she said. "I figure I have about a 50-50 shot."

"How many women are on the board?" I asked.

"Less than half," she said. "If they vote along gender lines, it won't go my way."

"Maybe one of the guys will flip. I'm sure you already have Beau's vote."

"True."

We left the resort parking lot and buzzed right into the heart of downtown Good Isle.

"This is a beautiful place," I said. "Even in winter it's probably gorgeous. You'll have to learn how to ski."

"I know how to ski," Ellen said. "Both downhill and cross country."

"Get out of here," I said. "When did you learn how to ski?"

She shook her head. "John, you really need to do a better job of keeping up with your only sibling."

We branched off from main street into a tree-lined street of picture-perfect old homes. The kind you see renovated on This Old House. They were colonials, most of them, but here and there were some stunning Victorians as well as the occasional bungalow.

The majority were immaculate and the ones that weren't seemed to be in the process of getting there.

"My kind of neighborhood," Ellen said.

I pulled up in front of a stunning house that wasn't full-on Victorian, but had some of that style's touches, like an ornate wraparound porch, fish scale siding, and a really cool turret.

"Very nice," Ellen observed. "I'm way more excited to go inside than I should be. Especially as we don't have permission from the owner."

"Well, his secret lover gave us permission so I don't have a problem with it," I said. "Then again, I'm a rebel."

"Rebel with a minivan," Ellen added.

I fished out the key Lindsey Nordegren had given me, locked up the minivan and stepped up onto the porch.

It was painted a light blue, and the railing was painted white. All of it fresh, and perfectly done.

Billy Dawkins was a man who liked nice things, and it appeared he had a passion for keeping them looking nice.

Not wanting to linger in full view of the neighbors, I put the key into the front door's lock. The door itself was a beauty. Solid, dark wood, with old-fashioned thick glass. The lock slid open soundlessly and I pushed it open. Ellen followed me inside and I closed the door quickly, locking it behind us.

"Oh my God," Ellen said.

CHAPTER THIRTEEN

"This is so nice," Ellen said. She looked at the hardwood floors, the perfectly refinished wood moldings, the leaded glass and was stunned. It was just about as perfect an old house as you could find.

"He is a meticulous man," John added.

Once through the small entrance, the house opened up into a central area with a staircase offset to the left, a hallway leading straight back, and two sets of French doors on either side. The glass in the French doors was breathtaking, at least an inch thick, beveled and in mint condition. They didn't make French doors like that anymore, Ellen knew from first-hand experience.

She opened the door to the right and walked into a parlor room, with a sitting area and a small fireplace surrounded by an elaborate, hand-carved wood mantle.

It was almost so pristine that she wondered if anyone lived here, let alone a man. So far, it almost felt like a museum.

Into the kitchen, which clearly wasn't original. Ellen knew most homes from the period had small kitchens, unlike the giant monstrosities most new construction featured. Nowadays, the huge, expansive kitchen that opened out into a family room was what everyone wanted.

This one was large, but not grotesquely so. There was a small eat-in space with a simple wooden table and four chairs. An original oil painting of a boxer hung to the right of the bay window that looked out into the backyard.

The counters were granite, the cabinets white and all of the appliances were stainless steel except for the fridge, which was faced with white that matched the cabinetry.

John entered from the other side of Ellen and she peeked out through that entrance. It was a formal dining room, with an elaborate Victorian dining set.

"This is the last kind of place I would expect a former boxer to own," John said. "There's gotta be a man cave downstairs or something, this doesn't even look like anyone lives here."

"Maybe he spent all of his time at his girlfriend's house," Ellen said. "Her husband was gone all the time, right?"

"Here, follow me," John said. He had found the door to the basement and she went down with him.

"Okay, this is more like it," he said.

The basement was divided in half. On one side was a full gym with free weights, weight machines and a heavy punching bag as well as a speed bag. Various jump ropes, training gloves and other exercise gear were all placed along one wall.

On the other side of the basement were all the mechanicals. The boiler, air conditioner and laundry area.

"Let's check out the upstairs," Ellen said.

She led the way to the staircase and up they went to a wide landing, with four doors spread out on either side of them.

"Four bedrooms?" John said, with surprise in his voice.

"Probably three and a bathroom," Ellen answered.

But she was wrong, too. It was three bedrooms and a library.

They saved the library for last.

The main bedroom definitely had seen use, and it was clearly a man's bedroom. Men's clothes were all hung neatly in the closet, and the bathroom was simple and clean. Ellen noted shaving cream and a razor on a small shelf next to the sink.

Like the downstairs, everything upstairs was showroom neat.

"Aha," John said.

Ellen joined him in the den.

"Yeah, this is more like it," she said.

Clearly, Billy "Dynamite" Dawkins had picked one room to be his own, and this was it. There was an empty glass next to a whiskey decanter, sitting on the wide wooden desk. A large, flat-screen television was in one corner and an expensive, brown leather couch with matching chairs faced the screen. On the table in front of the couch was a collection of sports magazines.

The walls were adorned with fight posters, all for some of Dynamite's biggest fights. Ellen recognized the names from the article she'd read on her iPad.

There were also several pairs of autographed boxing gloves hung on the wall.

Ellen went behind the desk and studied the papers there.

A letter caught her eye.

It was sitting to the right of the main pile of paper, as if Dynamite had just read it and set it aside.

The letterhead belonged to a law firm with an address in Detroit.

Ellen skimmed the letter until she got to the middle paragraph:

"...your decision to continue to ignore the repeated communications regarding this financial issue will lead to serious consequences on your behalf. You are in breach of contract with Motor City Boxing Promotions, LLC and at this time felony charges of obstruction of justice, delinquency and perhaps embezzlement are all within the realm of possibility. We urge you to remit the outstanding balance to this firm immediately. Failure to do so will result in criminal charges and most likely jail time..."

The letter went on to provide payment details. Ellen took out her phone and snapped a quick photo of the letter, which John had also read over her shoulder.

"Sounds serious," he said. "Serious enough for someone to want to grab him."

"Maybe," Ellen said. "But what do they get out of grabbing him? Unless he has the money on him and it didn't sound like he did. Just a bunch of fishing gear and a restored Ford Bronco. Doesn't sound like these guys would be happy with just that."

"I wonder how much the outstanding balance is," John said.

Ellen had speculated on that, too.

"Well, if this house is any indication," she said, "Billy "Dynamite" Dawkins is doing just fine for himself."

CHAPTER FOURTEEN

Billy Dawkins knew it was going to be bad.

It felt criminal to even refer to the motley group of rednecks before him as a crowd. They looked more like a bunch of genetic rejects forced to wear filthy clothing and live in the woods.

Oh, Dawkins had nothing against country folks. He'd been raised in the city, but plenty of people he'd gotten to know over the years were simple people who had turned out to be big fans of his.

But this element here was not a group of friendly, good-natured people.

They were like a wild pack of mongrels.

"Where is this bitch?" one of the men yelled and the group laughed.

Dawkins tried to take in his surroundings. He was even deeper into the woods than the last place. The trees here were thicker, packed more tightly together and a lot less light filtered in. It was near the end of the day, but inside the thick stand of forest, it already seemed dark.

What Dawkins also saw was a corrugated metal shed

surrounded by at least two dozen vehicles, most of them pickup trucks or some sort of 4x4. There were quite a few all-terrain vehicles and a motorcycle or two.

The group was exclusively male, as far as Billy could tell. A lot of camo clothing, ball caps, and people smoking cigarettes. There was also beer everywhere, guys chugging from cans and bottles.

Country music played in the background.

"Looks like your fan club is ready," Darnell said, shoving him forward.

Dawkins walked into the center of the clearing, spotted the door of the corrugated shed standing wide open. Inside, he could see a makeshift boxing ring.

"Let's get a good look at this sumbitch," one of them said. The eager ones sauntered up, beer cans in hand, and one of them spit a stream of chewing tobacco juice near his feet.

"This is it?" a guy with a T-shirt that said Get-r-done on the front scoffed at him. "You brought this weak-ass bitch up here to fight? I bet my old lady's got more kick than this mule hat's ready for the glue factory. Total lame-o."

Dawkins smiled. "Lame-o?"

Behind him, Troy gave him an extra sharp jab in the kidney with the end of the rifle.

"Shut up and keep walking."

The crowd parted way and Dawkins walked past them into the glorified storage shed. Immediately, what little light from the sun was blocked out, and someone flicked on an overhead light that was bright and more than a little harsh.

The whole place smelled like animals.

How appropriate, Dawkins thought.

Once inside, he got a good look at the ring, such as it was. There was one single line of rope, strung roughly into the shape of a square thanks to four metal fence posts pounded half-assed into the dirt floor.

One of the corners wasn't quite closed and Troy directed him through it.

The men from outside poured in, and Billy heard fresh beers being cracked, as well as bets being made.

Billy turned to face Troy and Darnell.

Darnell pulled out a big revolver. Stainless steel, with a huge barrel.

"Overcompensate much?" Dawkins asked him.

"Shut up," Darnell answered. "Unlock his cuffs."

Troy handed the rifle to a man next to him, who brought the butt up to his shoulder and aimed it directly at Billy's chest. Darnell backed up a step, and took careful aim at Dawkins's face.

"We're going to take those off, but you're here to fight," Darnell said. "You try to escape. You try to get one of us. You'll get shot and buried out here in the woods so no one will find what's left of your sorry ass."

"Lovely," Dawkins said. He held his hands out in front of him and Troy unlocked the cuffs.

His wrists were numb and he slowly flexed them up and down, trying to get some blood flow going. He needed to loosen up if he was going to fight someone.

"Where are they?" Darnell asked someone in the crowd.

"Just pulled up," a guy in back answered.

There was a series of hoots and hollers from outside the building and Billy figured his competition had arrived. He took the opportunity to step into the ring and look around. The man with the rifle had followed his every move, as had Darnell. The only door was the one they'd just come through. It didn't even have a side door.

A second group of men poured into the shed, and the last ones in were three big bodies, all about the same size, shape and appearance.

Brothers, Dawkins thought.

Three of them.

More whoops followed as Billy's three opponents took off their shirts, revealing muscular bodies. Not the low body fat types of physique seen on people in gyms, but the ham and butter-fed slabs of beef produced regularly in the upper Midwest.

These were farm boys.

Probably as strong as a team of oxen, and hopefully just as stupid.

Billy moved back into the ring as the three brothers entered, standing loosely apart. One of them smiled at him, revealing a row of yellow teeth that looked like seed corn.

Dawkins guessed each one of them weighed somewhere between 250 and 275. He himself had lost weight since his fighting days, and was now barely around 200.

He was outweighed and outmanned.

The bloodthirsty crowd surrounded the ring and began calling for the fight to start.

Dawkins did a quick assessment of the three brothers. They weren't triplets. They looked close in age, maybe two years apart. With the oldest in the middle. To the right of him was probably the youngest one, he had the most fire in his eye, eager to prove his mettle.

He would be the first to attack.

The oldest one would probably hang back, let his younger brothers take the initial abuse, and then try to be the one to finish him off.

A shot rang out and Darnell emerged from the crowd, the huge revolver sporting a tongue of smoke from its muzzle.

"At the next shot, the fight will start," he loudly proclaimed. "Dynamite, take off your shirt and let's see that old man's body we all know is hiding under there. Show us some man boobies."

The crowd erupted in laughter.

Dawkins had seen his share of street fights, but the thought of fighting without gloves pissed him off even more. His hands had seen a lot of work over the years and you could break a hand in a split second with the wrong kind of punch.

Still, he complied by taking off his shirt and enduring a bunch of catcalls at his expense.

"Damn, you gone soft, man!"

The fact was, he worked out four times a week and his routines included plenty of time on the heavy bag. But they were comparing him to his fighting days from a decade ago. When he was cut and in the prime of his life.

Well, someone had called him a mule. It was time to show them how hard he could hit.

He was now standing in one corner, and the three Farm Boy Brothers were spread out, the youngest one eager to come at him.

Darnell raised the revolver.

"You boys get ready for a helluva fight!"

The crowd erupted and more beers were cracked.

Darnell's finger pulled the trigger.

CHAPTER FIFTEEN

John and Ellen put together a plan, and most of the action items were assigned to him.

"Sorry, but I can't go sticking my nose too far into this case," Ellen said. "At least, not until I find out what the committee decides. If they make me an offer and it's a good one, I don't want to get into trouble for being involved in a local investigation before I even join the force."

"You and your rules," John said. "You need to learn to live a little."

"You and your penchant for breaking the rules," she countered.

Ellen sensed the draw of the private investigator, though. It was liberating to be able to go where you wanted, follow whatever lead you felt was the strongest, and not have to deal with office politics. And following procedure. When you had enemies in the office, the slightest breach of protocol could be deadly.

If you were a lone wolf private investigator, none of that bullshit applied.

But she was born to be a police officer, and she'd never turn in the badge of her own accord.

"Why don't you follow up on the Motor City Promotions angle, and I'll look into the Detroit law firm," Ellen said. "I know exactly who to call for information, because I've heard of that group before. And I don't think it was positive."

They talked over theories on the way to the resort, and then agreed to meet later for dinner, depending on what they found.

Ellen returned to her room.

As much as she liked the resort, and the room was very spacious with a great view, she missed her house. She missed her own bed, her own kitchen, and her own space.

Why am I up here interviewing for a job then? she asked herself.

Great question.

She felt a little tired and debated about taking a nap or getting a workout in.

As usual, the workout won.

She put on a pair of tennis shoes, shorts and a T-shirt, and went down to the resort's fitness center. After a good forty-five minutes on the treadmill, she did a quick routine with free weights and then returned to her room for a hot shower and a change of clothes for dinner later.

Ellen dug through her phone and found an old friend who worked as an attorney downtown. His name was Colin Dougherty. After an exchange of pleasantries, Ellen brought up the name of the firm that had sent the threatening letter to Dawkins.

Colin let out a low whistle.

"Stay away from those guys," Dougherty said. "They're bad, bad news."

"Bad news in what way?"

"Utterly ruthless in court," Doughtery answered. "Known

for intimidating witnesses and using less than savory methods to get witnesses to either appear, or not appear, depending on what side they're on."

"Yikes."

"And that's not even the worst part."

"Great."

"Have you seen the movie The Firm?"

"Sure," Ellen replied. "Tom Cruise. The fake law firm owned by..." she realized what she was about to say and stopped herself.

"Yep. The rumor is they're at least partly owned by the Mob," Dougherty said, his voice suddenly low and quiet. "So trust me, Ellen, you really, really don't want to get involved with them."

They agreed to meet in a week or two for drinks and then Ellen disconnected from the call.

Well, it wasn't that big of a surprise. The sport of boxing and the Mafia have always been linked, due to the gambling nature of the enterprise. Throwing fights, taking dives, it was all on the table, which is partly why the sport had lost so much of its luster over the years.

Her phone rang and she saw it was John.

"Gosh that was a good nap," he said. "I suppose you worked out."

He knew her very well.

"What's up?" she asked. She checked her watch. Still a little early for dinner.

"The girls and Anna have apparently booked a reservation at some dinner theater at the edge of town," he said "It's some kind of Sesame Street show or something. I said you were busy on the case, like I am, and can't go. So, you're off the hook for dinner tonight."

A part of her wouldn't have minded seeing it, just for giggles. But depending on what news she may or may not hear, there was an opportunity to go downtown again and sample some of Good Isle's best restaurants.

"Okay," she said. "Let me tell you what I found out."

She filled him on the law firm and its reputation.

"Huh," he said.

There were voices in the background and then John said, "All right, Ellen. I gotta run. Have fun in Good Isle. They probably roll up the sidewalks at 8 p.m. so you'd better hurry."

She ended the call and slid the phone into her purse.

A night on the town in Good Isle seemed interesting.

She left the resort, went out to her car and drove downtown. Traffic was a little heavier so it took five minutes instead of four.

Ellen parked along a row of shops she'd seen earlier and made her way along the sidewalk, checking out the merchandise and the prices. Some of the tags listed a pretty high price and she wondered if she'd underestimated what the cost of living might be up here.

Down from the shops, she came across a restaurant and bar with the name of Sullivan's. Through the window, she could see a bar and dining room that was filling up fast.

She was about to go in when she heard a voice behind her.

"Ellen Rockne?"

She turned and saw a woman in a police uniform approaching her. A squad car was double parked next to the curb.

"Yes," Ellen said.

The woman stopped in front of her.

"You're under arrest."

CHAPTER SIXTEEN

It was a touch late for a quick call to Nate, but I'd done some research back at the hotel while Anna and the girls got ready for their Sesame Street show. I was disappointed I couldn't go, especially because the Cookie Monster was one of my favorite childhood characters.

He and I ate cookies exactly the same way.

With two hands, crumbs cascading down onto our chest.

Especially if they were chocolate chip.

Nate answered immediately.

"Where are you?" he asked. "I dropped by your office today."

"Up north, in Good Isle. Why were you paying me a visit?"

"Just wanted to see if you were up for lunch, but you weren't," he said, with a tired, disappointed sigh. "What are you doing up there?"

I hesitated. I trusted Nate with my life, but I was also cognizant of the fact that my sister was currently employed by the City of Grosse Pointe, and was semi-actively pursuing a job in Good Isle.

It wouldn't be good for that news to get out.

"Ellen somehow got an extra room on her trip up here so she invited us up for a long weekend."

"What's Ellen doing up there?" Nate, the intrepid reporter, loved asking questions.

I kicked myself for even mentioning her name.

"Some kind of law enforcement seminar or something, I don't know," I said. "I just made sure the room was free."

Nate grunted.

A part of me hoped Ellen didn't get the job, because if she did, and took it, I would have to admit to Nate that I lied about why she was up in Good Isle.

Oh, the tangled web we weave.

"Hey, I've got a quick question for you," I said, wanting to change the subject as quickly as possible. "Ever heard of a company called Motor City Boxing Promotions? I did some Internet sleuthing and saw that their name was on some fights a decade or so ago."

"Sure, that's Don White's company," Nate said. "You know who Don White is?"

I did. I had done some research based on the letter from the Detroit law firm about breach of contract, and learned that Don White had been Billy Dawkins's manager.

Now, I had a nice connection.

"He managed a lot of Detroit fighters back when boxing was pretty big in the city."

"Guys like Dynamite Dawkins, right?" I asked.

"Yep, Dynamite was probably his most well-known fighter. Came within one challenger of a shot at the title. Fucked up his eye then, and it was all she wrote."

I could almost hear Nate's brain making connections over the phone.

"Wait a minute," he said. "Doesn't Dynamite live up in

Good Isle now? Holy shit. Are you working a case involving him? What happened?"

"Whoa, whoa, whoa, Tiger," I said. "I'm just checking on something for a friend while I'm here on vacation." It wasn't really a lie. Lindsey Nordegren and I were technically acquaintances now, which was close enough to the friend label for me.

"Hmmm," Nate said. "Well, I think you're full of shit, like always, John. But a word of warning. Don White and his crew are not to be trifled with. Motor City Boxing was rumored to be involved with all kinds of questionable characters back in the day, if you know what I mean."

"Yeah, well, do you remember freshman year in high school? My fight with Ted Wilson?"

"Oh my God," Nate said. "You are a sad, sad man."

My victory over a five-second fist fight in high school was something I always liked to bring up to Nate whenever he questioned my obvious machismo.

"He never saw that punch coming," I said. "I've always had tremendous knockout power. With each hand."

Nate hung up on me, which was fine. Envy can ruin friendships and it was better if Nate dealt with his own issues on his time.

During my research, I had come across an article about Don White and his extensive collection of restored Chris-Craft wooden boats. They were legendary watercraft, started in Michigan back in the early 20th century and were prized by collectors. The article stated that Don White, a resident of Blue Harbor, Michigan, owned some of the finest examples in the Midwest.

Blue Harbor was only an hour north of Good Isle, and I wondered who had settled in the area first; Don White or Billy Dawkins? I'm sure it wasn't coincidence that a fighter and his manager ended up buying homes within an hour of each other.

Another trip onto the Internet and an address database revealed Don White's home address in Blue Harbor. I used Google Maps to check it out, and he lived in one of the waterfront mansions I'd seen on my drive with Ellen.

Every town along Lake Michigan's shoreline had its own stretch of mansions. In fact, you could pretty much drive from the bottom of the state to the top along the shoreline, where most of the real estate was devoted to very nice homes.

And lots of produce stands.

Anna and the girls were using Uber to get to the play, which shocked me that the small town of Good Isle even had the car service, but there you go.

You can't stop progress, can you?

So, I fired up the minivan, headed north out of Good Isle and was treated to a spectacular sunset drive. The steep bluffs hid the view from drivers on the road, until you crested the top, and then the beauty of Lake Michigan hit you in the face like a right cross from Dynamite Dawkins.

It was breathtaking, and now, with the fading sun settling below the western horizon, the sky was a masterpiece of oranges, reds and deep pinks. I suddenly wished I was a painter and could reproduce sunsets like this so I could have a permanent record. Paintings, especially impressionist pieces, were more moving to me than photographs.

Eventually the narrow ribbon of highway rolled down into Blue Harbor, a town that matched Good Isle in its postcard-quality setting.

In fact, it felt like almost a mirror image of Good Isle, with the requisite outer strip of retail stores before hitting the historic section downtown, and of course, the harbor. I turned left in town, and wound my way along the lake.

Again, the amount of money invested in waterfront real

estate, even in these small towns along Lake Michigan was astounding.

I wasn't a jealous man, but I did wonder how many doctors, lawyers and CEOs there could possibly be to merit the hundreds and hundreds of million-dollar estates.

Of course, not all of the folks living in these Architectural Digest properties traded among those professions. Don White, for instance, was a boxing manager.

And, as I gazed upon his home, clearly new construction done in the style of a traditional Michigan farmhouse on steroids, I guessed he was one of the more successful promoters of his kind.

I turned the minivan assertively into his driveway and drove up to the house.

My shoes tread soundlessly as I climbed the stairs of the front porch that somehow was obviously built recently, yet at the same time felt quaintly rustic.

It was amazing what enough money could do.

I was about to ring the doorbell when a loud noise erupted from the rear of the house.

The noise I recognized immediately.

It was a gunshot.

CHAPTER SEVENTEEN

As it turned out, they came at him exactly the way Dawkins had expected.

Youngest to oldest.

The young one, full of an inferiority complex or eagerness to prove he was tougher than his older brothers, raced across the makeshift ring, faked a straight left and then threw a murderous haymaker with his right.

Dawkins saw it coming a mile away.

Rather than duck away from the feint, he stepped closer at the obvious jab, inside the haymaker, and threw a short right with everything he had. Dawkins torqued his body and drove his fist into, and then through, the younger brother's chin.

The young man's head snapped and the sound was like an axe splitting a massive piece of firewood.

Dawkins saw the man's lights go out. He leaned forward, his jaw loose, probably broken, and toppled forward, landing in the dirt on his face.

The crowd fell silent.

Dawkins couldn't dwell on the success of his first punch

because the middle brother was right behind the first attacker.

Unlike his predecessor, this one made no attempt to hide what he was doing. Dawkins remembered that middle children were often indecisive and failed to form their own opinions. They were followers. Not leaders. One of the negatives of being in the middle of the birth order.

That dynamic seemed to play itself out right before his eyes.

Because the middle brother's clear intent was to tackle him, get him to the ground, and probably hold him down while the senior brother pounded his face into a bloody pulp.

The great thing about his background, however, was that Dawkins hadn't only been trained in the ring. In fact, he'd grown up on the streets and learned the ins and outs of fighting the hard way.

Namely, by getting his ass kicked constantly.

So, when Middle Brother came at him, head down, arms outstretched to tackle him, Dawkins used a little bit of a Muay Thai technique. He sprung forward and brought his knee up with as much force as possible.

He didn't time it perfectly, however, and instead of catching the attacker under the chin, it arrived too early, scraped up the man's lips and smashed into his nose, ripping the cartilage loose and sending a spray of blood into the air.

He kept coming, though, and crashed into Dawkins, sending both of them to the ground.

Dawkins knew he only had a split second to escape or he'd have a combined weight of five hundred pounds on top of him, ready to pulverize him.

He rolled to the right, out from under the body of the dazed middle brother, and started to get to his feet. Someone from the crowd punched him in the back of the neck and it momentarily caused him to shift his weight, which ended up being a good thing because the first brother was now in front of him, throwing a straight right that missed its mark because of the punch from behind.

Too many cooks in the kitchen, Dawkins thought.

The blow caught the side of Billy's neck and part of his ear, glancing off the corner of the rear jaw.

Still, it straightened him up and he felt his first flash of pain.

The blood rage was in him now, and he forgot about his age, the setting and what might happen afterward.

Now, he wanted to destroy.

He bent at the knees and threw his own straight right directly into the first brother's midsection.

A beautiful body blow that stunned his opponent, who instinctively lowered his arms, which was what Dawkins had hoped he would do.

This gave him the perfect window of opportunity to throw a short left that landed on the button and made Brother #1 lift his arms back up.

Dawkins responded with a perfectly thrown right hook that was loaded with the kind of explosive power that had earned him his nickname.

He felt the man's ribs crack and he knew he'd broken more than one. The man went to his knees so Dawkins repeated the same punch, except now it nearly took his opponent's head right off.

By now, the middle brother was back on his feet, his face and chest covered in blood from a nose that was barely hanging onto his face.

Dawkins smiled and advanced on him. He'd forgotten how much he loved to fight and now, he was thoroughly enjoying being back in the ring.

Fear covered the man's face. Both of his brothers were out of it, and he was now facing a man who had a reputation as pound for pound the hardest hitting boxer who'd ever graced the canvas.

Dawkins could tell he wanted out, but there was no way out, for either one of them.

First Dawkins jabbed, a feint that caused the man to duck just in time for a beautiful uppercut that connected squarely under the chin. In the room, which had gone suddenly very quiet once again, it sounded like a poleax crashing into the skull of a cow.

Ten years ago, that would have been the end of the fight, Dawkins knew. As vicious as his punches still were, they weren't of the quality from his glory days.

He stepped in and threw a combination of punches, the last one being a roundhouse right that knocked the man out on his feet.

Dawkins's last opponent was swaying on his feet and Billy knew it would take one easy punch to finish it.

So instead, he kicked him in the balls.

Hey, no rules in this kind of fight.

Dawkins had decided that clowns like this forfeited their right to breed.

Down in the dirt he went and Dawkins turned to the crowd.

He was sweating and his breath was coming quickly. But he had never stopped training, and now it had paid off.

He caught the eye of Darnell, who was approaching him from the corner of the ring.

Instead of the giant revolver in his hand, he had a metal rod of some sort.

"Who's next?" Dawkins asked.

He was warmed up, and angry, and the blood thirst was in him.

Darnell jabbed him with the end of the rod, which Dawkins realized too late was a cattle prod.

Fifty thousand volts went through him and he sagged to the ground. The last thing he saw was all of the men converging on him, cracking their knuckles.

Darnell smiled and the last thing Dawkins heard was the answer to his question.

"All of us," he said.

CHAPTER EIGHTEEN

"Just kidding," the woman said. "You're not under arrest."

She stuck out her hand. "Maddie Burfict."

Ellen was struck by the woman's physique. She must have been a bodybuilder because even through the police uniform, never the most flattering attire, Ellen could make out the serious muscles. Arms, legs, even the cords in her neck looked impressive.

"Ellen Rockne."

"You sure are," Officer Burfict said. "I got a sneak peek at the people who they're considering for chief, and you popped right out at me. I couldn't imagine a woman being the chief of Police in Good Isle."

Burfict smiled, revealing a perfect set of very white teeth, which seemed even brighter because of the tan skin. Had to be a tanning booth in Good Isle, Ellen thought.

Ellen didn't care for the message the woman was conveying, though. "I'm sure there are a lot of people who couldn't imagine a female police chief, they probably said the same thing about letting women vote."

Burfict cocked her head to the side. "I think I might like you."

A couple emerged from the restaurant behind them and did a double take when they saw a police officer. Ellen wondered if they were hoping they'd see an arrest. Maybe two women fighting it out on the street would be their free, evening entertainment.

"Because I like you, I hope you don't get the job," Burfict said. "Sorry to be blunt. But it's more like babysitting than actual police work. Not like down in Grosse Pointe. You get a lot of spillover action from Detroit, right?"

"I guess it depends what you mean by spillover action. What is that?"

"You know, guns, drugs, murder. That kind of thing."

Ellen studied the woman before her a bit more closely. She had a strong jaw, smooth skin that was flawless, and light brown hair. Her eyes were dark and wide, and when she spoke, her thin lips only parted slightly.

This was a woman who cared a great deal about her appearance. And it showed.

"Oh, Grosse Pointe has long stretches of boredom, too," Ellen said evenly. "And that's the way most Grosse Pointers like it."

"Yeah, but do the cops like it?"

"Most of the officers in my department have families," Ellen explained. "Their kids go to Grosse Pointe schools, so I would say yes. They prefer to have a quiet, safe community."

Officer Burfict blew a big, pink bubble and let it pop.

Ellen hadn't even realized the woman was chewing gum.

"I'm probably over exaggerating how quiet it is here," Burfict said. "Occasionally we get some crazy shit going on, mostly from the areas east of here. Meth dealers. Weed growers. A few militia members. Actually, one of the militia guys is pretty well-connected. John Harrison probably already knows who the committee is considering for chief of police. Hell, he probably knows who you are."

This woman is interesting, Ellen thought. What was she saying? That the head of a criminal militia had a file on her? Trying to scare her away?

"Well, I've gotta run, I'm on duty," Burfict said. She stuck out her hand and Ellen shook it. This time, the cop gave it an extra firm squeeze.

It felt like a vice grip to Ellen.

"Good luck, maybe I'll see you around up here," Burfict said.

"Yeah, we'll see," Ellen answered.

Officer Burfict got back in her squad car and cruised past Ellen, giving a little wave as she went by.

What was that all about?

Ellen figured that Maddie Burfict had spent time scouring Good Isle to see if she could meet up with the woman who was being considered for chief of police and could potentially be her new boss. She had probably driven out to the resort, and then figured Ellen would come downtown in the evening where she could accidentally "bump into" her. Say hello, maybe scare her off? Or just check her out?

Ellen decided the best approach would be to go into the restaurant, take a seat at the bar and consider it some more over a dirty martini.

She did just that and was offered a high-top table to the right of the main bar.

It was quiet, only three other people in the bar. Two of them constituted a couple who looked like they were about to head into the restaurant area and wolf down some fried fish. The third person was a single man with thick black hair and a matching beard. He had on a Hawaiian shirt, jeans and flip flops. Probably late thirties or early forties. Ellen knew he had used the mirror behind the bar to watch her come in.

Ellen slid her cell phone out from her purse and dialed John.

"Good thing you called," he said before she could even get a word out. "Someone just fired a gun."

"Probably deer hunters."

"Mm, I don't think so. It sounds like it came from the backyard of Don White's house. He used to be Dynamite's manager. I'm going to check it out."

"Don't get shot."

"I'll try not to. No promises, though."

"Have you heard of Michigan's militia movement?" Ellen asked.

"This isn't a great time, Ellen."

"I know, but I've got something for you."

"Okay, hold on."

Ellen heard a car door shut.

"All right, I'm in my car. Go ahead."

"Michigan militias."

"Sure, everyone knows Michigan is home to crazy-ass guys who love going into the woods with guns and want nothing to do with the government," John said. "Except at the cherry festivals, then they come in and eat cherry pie all day."

"Well, I just heard that the local militia is run by a guy named John Harrison. Apparently, he's got his finger on the pulse of Good Isle and knows what everyone's doing all the time."

"Does he know I'm wearing pink silk underwear right now?"

Ellen pulled the phone away from her ear and looked at it. Finally, she returned it to her ear.

"You are getting stranger and stranger the more you age," she said.

"Thank you. You said John Harrison is his name?"

"Yeah."

"And you're telling me this just in case my other leads on Dynamite Dawkins go nowhere."

"Yes."

"Okay, duly noted. Now I have to go see somebody about a gunshot."

Ellen glanced up and saw the guy at the bar was coming toward her table.

"That's right, I'm out on parole for the weekend," she said quite loudly into the phone, even though John had already hung up. "And then it's back in the slammer on Monday."

The man from the bar adjusted course and walked past her, detouring to the men's room.

Ellen smiled, drained the rest of her martini, and paid her bill.

She walked out into the early evening.

It had been enough fun for one night.

Good night, Good Isle.

CHAPTER NINETEEN

I disconnected from the call with Ellen and got out of the minivan.

There was no doubt in my mind the shot was from behind the house. I walked up the driveway, went to the right of the home, and followed the drive back toward the garage, which wasn't attached but was still done in the style of the main home.

As I walked, I thought about the possibility of getting shot. No two ways about it, I didn't want to get shot.

Bullets and John Rockne don't mix well.

I'd found that out the hard way.

Now, I passed the bulk of the house, peeking in one of the windows and recognized a beautiful, gleaming kitchen.

No one was inside, though.

As I rounded the corner of the house, the first thing I noticed was the pool. It was huge, with one long lane running down the middle, opening up into an extended area at the other end. My guess is someone wanted the luxury of swimming a true Olympic length pool, so they'd built the pool to accommodate that wish.

You'd have to swim through the party end of the pool, but I figured it was the owner who'd requested it and the guests would probably get the hell out of the way.

The second thing that appeared was a man dressed in a tiny swimming suit, holding a shotgun, while a woman threw clay pigeons into the air.

"Pull!" he shouted.

The woman, with skin the color of flawless ebony countered by her hot pink bikini, threw the clay pigeon into the air.

The man blasted it out of the sky, and I noticed that when the shotgun recoiled, the man's blubbery body seemed to ripple with the blast. This was the kind of man whose body should never sport a tiny swimming suit.

He needed some of those huge surfer shorts and a baggy T-shirt.

But this? It wasn't a pretty sight.

"Pull!"

The gun boomed.

"Pull!"

The gun boomed again.

"Pull!"

The gun went click.

"19 for 20!" the man bellowed. "Shit, I was on fire!"

"You sure were, Daddy," the black woman in the bikini said. "Your shit was on fire!"

She went up to him and gave him a huge kiss and their tongues wrestled in each other's mouths for a full thirty seconds before the woman noticed me standing there.

She winked at me, peeled herself away from the man and took a running dive into the swimming pool.

The man must have sensed my presence because he turned, and I inadvertently flinched as the end of the shotgun was briefly pointing at me.

"Who the hell are you?" he asked.

I walked tentatively closer to him. He looked even bigger and fatter the closer I got.

"John Rockne. I'm looking for Don White."

The man dropped the shotgun to the ground, which seemed incredibly careless and dangerous. Not exactly the picture of gun safety.

"What for?" he said.

He walked over to a table by the edge of the pool and picked up a glass of brown liquor. Probably scotch if I had to guess.

I got a good look at him and he was a big man, his face florid, with white hair tied back into a small pony tail. He had thin legs, topped by a huge, overhanging torso. A gold chain hung down into his gray, curly chest hair.

"I have some questions about Billy Dynamite Dawkins."

"Dynamite Dawkins? Is he still alive?"

He smiled and his teeth were yellow and crooked. Probably a cigar smoker.

"I believe so, yes," I answered.

"Who the hell is John Rockne?" he asked me. "Never heard of you."

"I'm from Grosse Pointe. Just a big fan of Dynamite's and I know you used to be his manager."

"If you're one of them memorabilia leeches, I don't have any of his shit. No one does. The guy's old news, washed up, never got a shot at the title."

He scoffed.

"So you are Don White, correct?" I asked.

"No, I'm Captain Kangaroo," he snarled at me. "Of course I am! Christ, are you stupid?"

The black woman was swimming laps and I watched her arms slice through the water with power and precision.

"You look like a reporter," he said to me, his voice full of suspicion. "Are you a reporter?"

White's eyes looked at me with anger and derision.

"No, I'm a private investigator."

"A PI? Why the hell is a PI looking for Dawkins?"

"Just a concerned friend, that's all. Have you see him?"

"I haven't spoken to him in years," White said. "We had a falling out because he's a giant asshole. Tried to rip me off but I've got some good lawyers. If you do find him, tell him I hope he rots in hell."

"Do you know anyone who would want to hurt him?" I asked. "Or who had a beef with him?" And then I added, "Besides you."

"Jesus Christ, everyone did! People lost tons of money betting on him. I worked my ass off for that jerk and then he bailed on me. Backed out of a huge fight. Cost me a fortune."

White stuck his hand inside his swimming suit and scratched himself. I suddenly wanted to throw up.

"Detached retina, wasn't it?" I asked. "That's why Dawkins retired?"

"That pussy was detached from his balls, more like it," White said.

The black woman in the pool cackled.

White smiled at her.

"Like that one, Kezie?"

"I did, Daddy. That was funny as shit!"

White got up, went over to the shotgun and picked it up. He loaded more shells into the shotgun and then again carelessly pointed it in my direction.

"Goodbye, Mr. Rockne."

I backed away and made it back to my minivan before I heard the shotgun blast again.

"Pull!"

CHAPTER TWENTY

By the time I made it back to Good Isle, it was late and I thought about going to the hotel bar for a drink, but decided otherwise.

I texted Anna, and considered meeting them at their Sesame Street show, but she replied that they were on their way back.

That meant I had enough time to get back to the room and check my email. There was nothing of interest there and I was reading an article about Don White when Anna and the girls piled in.

We spent the next hour or so listening to the girls recounting and re-enacting their favorite parts of the show.

I didn't think they'd ever sleep, but eventually it was lights out, and Anna was the first one asleep. I ended up dreaming about diving into Don White's pool only to be shot by a shotgun in mid-air and landing in my own pool of blood.

The next morning, I was back at the investigation, hoping that something would break loose because Anna and the girls were going to have to head back to Grosse Pointe, which meant I would need to get a hotel room and pay for it, as well as a rental car.

It wasn't going to be easy to find the local militia.

How does one go about it?

It's not like they have an army base with a guard at the gate. What I was fairly certain of was that most guys in a militia didn't do it as a full-time job. Therefore, they had to earn their paychecks somewhere.

I suspected John Harrison wasn't any different.

At first, I thought I had gotten lucky and it was going to be easy. There was a Harrison Hardware store smack dab in the middle of Good Isle. I left the resort after breakfast, went directly to the store and asked to speak with John Harrison.

Turns out the store had nothing to do with John Harrison.

Even worse, the person I spoke to, a young man with a goatee and a Detroit Lions baseball cap, seemed to have very little interest in telling me where I might be able to find him. The only reason that asking seemed like a good idea was that with Good Isle being a small town, they had to occasionally have been asked if they were related to "that" John Harrison.

Next stop was the public library. Easy option first. I went to the information desk and asked for information on John Harrison, head of the local militia.

The old lady, quite pretty in a blue sweater and crisp khaki pants, looked at me with an odd expression.

Next option, not so easy.

The local papers had to have written a news story on the local militia. It was always required, at least once a year, to check in with the crazies and see what they were up to.

I signed up for Internet usage, and logged into a special database of collated news stories and searched using John Harrison's name and keywords like Michigan, militia, right-wing, Good Isle, soldiers, and so on.

Eventually, I found what I was looking for.

An article by the main paper in Traverse City, which was south of Good Isle, covering the rise of a small but reportedly powerful group called the Good Isle Militia. The story referenced John Harrison, owner of Good Furniture, a builder of custom furniture with a shop located on the outskirts of Good Isle, along Highway 31.

I wondered how many businesses in the area used the same trick with the name.

Good Groceries.

Good Sperm Bank.

Good Roach Killers.

I checked my watch, estimated how long it would take me to get to Good Furniture and sent Anna a text. I figured I had just enough time to drive out and talk to Mr. Harrison, that is, if he wasn't out in the woods trying to plan the attack on Grand Rapids.

That way, I could get back to the resort and figure out if Anna was taking the van and I was going to stay in Good Isle and continue my efforts to find Billy "Dynamite" Dawkins.

Out of the library, back on the road.

It was a gray day, overcast, with occasional splatters of rain. It did nothing to diminish the beauty of the place, though. The rolling hills and occasional steep bluff were shrouded in clouds, making the geography feel like a bit of Ireland come to the Midwest.

I had to use the van's wipers occasionally, and I drove by the furniture store twice before I finally found it.

It wasn't really a store as much as a garage. I pulled off the highway, after finally spotting the Good Furniture sign, and parked. It was literally a detached garage, with a farmhouse set back from the road.

I heard the sound of saws and caught a whiff of sawdust. A rocking chair with narrow spindles sat just outside the door.

As I stepped up to the entrance, I checked the price tag on the chair.

Seven hundred bucks.

It all depended if it was handmade. If so, that wasn't a bad price. If it was assembled using a bunch of prefabricated chunks of inferior wood or particleboard? Not so much.

I stepped into the room and saw stacks of wood, half-finished projects, and a big shelf with an assortment of stains and varnishes. A clock hung over the desk with the words "Got Wood?"

Great question.

A man shut off the table saw in back, and I saw him take off his safety goggles.

He walked up toward me and he looked like a young Harrison Ford. Tall, rangy, good-looking.

There was a twinkle in his eye and he smiled at me.

"You must be John Rockne," he said.

CHAPTER TWENTY-ONE

"So it's true," I said.

Harrison smiled at me, knowing where I was going with it.

"You do know everything that goes on in Good Isle," I said, repeating what Ellen had told me, that the head of the local militia was better informed than the area news organizations.

Harrison wiped a thin line of sweat that was beading up along his forehead. Apparently building furniture was hard work.

"Oh that's, what do you call it, an urban myth," he said. "Although, using the word 'urban' in Good Isle seems a little incongruous."

Now it was my turn to be surprised. I figured Harrison was going to be an up-north shitkicker. He seemed well-spoken and intelligent.

"Looks like you've got some beautiful stuff here," I said, looking around his showroom. "I knew someone who used to build guitars from logs that had sunk to the bottom of Lake Michigan."

He nodded. "Beautiful stuff. Problem is, very few people can afford it. A chest of drawers made from that stuff would cost about twenty grand."

"Only so many Warren Buffetts in the world," I pointed out.

"And Warren Buffett would never buy one. The guy's worth a billion and still lives in a little three-bedroom house in Omaha."

Good Isle was just full of surprises. The head of the local militia was a custom furniture maker and a student of Warren Buffett's, apparently. You never could judge a book by its cover these days.

"So how can I help you?" he asked me. "Other than telling you where Dynamite Dawkins is because I have no idea."

This time, the smile turned into a laugh.

"You're really enjoying this, aren't you?" I asked.

"Sort of."

It gave me pause. Did he know about Dawkins and Lindsey Nordegren? I had to assume so, but I didn't want to ask him. Besides, it didn't really matter if he did. The main thing was finding the fighter.

"Yes, I am trying to find Dynamite Dawkins. Are you sure you don't know where he is?"

He shrugged his shoulders.

"More importantly, do you think your sister will take the job if she's offered it?" he asked.

"Jesus Christ!" I practically spit it out. "What are you, clairvoyant?"

"It's a small town, man. People talk."

"What are they saying about Dynamite Dawkins?"

It was an obvious ploy to get the conversation back to the topic at hand. I needed to find Dawkins and get him in touch with Lindsey Nordegren. That way I could get paid and get back to my life in Grosse Pointe. As much as I

enjoyed the north woods, I couldn't spend the next
month here.

Harrison nodded toward a pair of chairs near the front of
the garage. We each took a seat.

He looked at me.

"My Dad told me something once," he said. "One of the
few things he ever said that made sense to me. He told me
that the physical act of sex was no different than having a
highly satisfying bowel movement."

"Wow, that's romantic," I said. "You should go work for
Hallmark."

"He conveyed that nugget of wisdom to me when I was a
young man because he'd seen too many people throw their
lives away over a couple of hot nights between the sheets
with a nimble young woman."

"Story of my life," I said.

"Seems like some guys never understand that," Harrison
said. He wiped away some of the dust on his jeans. "Even
when they're not young anymore."

He looked up at me to make sure I understood he was
talking about Dynamite Dawkins and Lindsay Nordegren. So
he knew about them, too.

I was about to ask him another question when we both
heard a loud vehicle pull up to the entrance of the shop.

Harrison looked out to see who it was.

Well, I had my answer.

He certainly did know about Dawkins and Lindsey. Hell,
the whole town probably knew about it. That discussion at
Beau's house, in retrospect, seemed ridiculous. Trying to keep
a secret that wasn't a secret.

My employers were wasting their time and frankly, it was
possibly time to go to the police. I had half a mind to go back
to my clients and tell them having me chase down Dawkins

secretly was a waste of time, especially since the whole town knew he was going extra rounds with another man's wife.

That meant all fingers were pointing at Lindsey's husband. It was the obvious place to look, which meant I had to confirm that he was actually out of the country like she said.

A door slammed outside and a guy appeared in the doorway of the shop.

He was a well-built guy, young, in jeans and a long-sleeved flannel shirt. He had on a cowboy hat and mirrored sunglasses.

"What's up?" Harrison asked him.

The man glanced over at me, or at least I guess he did because I couldn't see his eyes, but the direction of his head indicated he had looked me over.

"Same old," he replied.

Harrison pointed at me.

"This is John Rockne," he said.

And then he pointed at the new arrival.

"John, this is Darnell."

CHAPTER TWENTY-TWO

Beatings were nothing new to Dynamite Dawkins.

In fact, it wasn't until he truly learned how to fight, to properly defend himself, that the ass-kickings had finally stopped.

And it hadn't just been learning the mechanics of fighting. How to throw a punch. How to convincingly bluff a jab, or counter a body shot.

No, even more important had been learning the strategy of a fight.

To strike first.

Do the unexpected.

Show no mercy.

Those were things he'd had to learn, usually the hard way.

But before that, well, he'd climbed his way out of unconsciousness to find himself beaten, bloody and battered.

Just like now.

The man formerly known as Dynamite was a complete mess.

He knew it.

Hell, he could taste it.

Nothing tasted quite like blood. That metallic, smoky, almost sickly sweet flavor made his stomach turn. Not just because it was blood, but because it was his own.

He could tell his face was misshapen. His lips were blubbery, his tongue was cut, and his jaw hurt on both sides.

It wasn't broken, though.

He'd had that experience before and so he knew how to judge. Dawkins understood he had taken some vicious blows to the face, but at least the jaw was intact. Having a broken jaw was a devastating injury.

One eye was partially closed, his nose was possibly broken but he couldn't be sure without a mirror. For sure, he was having some trouble breathing.

"Jesus, you sound like gut-shot deer," a voice said next to him.

Dawkins slowly rotated his head, which caused shooting pains and a crushing ache from the top of his head all the way down through his body.

It was Troy. Sitting there with a shit-eating green on his face and holding a can of Mountain Dew.

The rifle was leaning up against his chair.

Across the room, a television was on and Dawkins realized Troy was watching the television and his captive at the same time. Hillbilly multi-tasking at its finest.

"Water," Dawkins barely managed to say. His voice sounded hoarse and the word was garbled.

"Yeah, I suppose you need something to wash all that blood down the hatch," Troy said, and then let out a little giggle.

He got up and took the rifle with him. When he returned, he had a Camelbak water bottle. He tossed it onto Dawkins's chest.

It hurt.

Dawkins winced and Troy laughed.

His hands were in cuffs once again, but he was able to lift the bottle and drink. He swirled the water around inside his broken mouth and let some drip onto his face. The cold felt good on what must have been a patchwork of bruises and swelling.

"Gotta tell you," Troy said as he sagged back into his chair. "A lotta boys lost money betting on the Carey brothers. No one thought you could take them down. That might be why some of them boys got a little carried away after Darnell zapped you with the cattle prod."

Troy giggled again and as much as he hurt, Dawkins would have loved to get his hands on him.

He forced himself to think.

As bad as the beating had been, he knew it could have been a lot worse. The problem was, he knew this wasn't the end.

Whoever was behind this had clearly set up a fight with some locals, and been paid to do it. Dawkins had heard all about illegal fight clubs, unsanctioned, with big dollars floating around. There were even leagues, as far as he'd heard. A big one in the south that included Texas, Oklahoma and New Orleans. Bare knuckle boxing matches, set up out in the woods.

The only difference was the fighters in those got paid, too.

Now, he was being forced to fight, or get shot.

He considered the option of not fighting. But he knew with that last crowd, they probably would've killed him. Even though at some point he lost consciousness, Dawkins guessed that Darnell had stopped the mob from killing him.

Because there was going to be another fight.

There was no way it would stop, after the kind of money he'd seen being tossed around before and during the fight.

Darnell had gotten a taste of being a fight promoter, seen the easy money, and would want to do it again.

Greed was something you could always count on.

In fact, he guessed that's where Darnell was now. Getting the word out, setting up another fight. They'd probably feed him, make sure he wasn't busted up too bad, and keep him going. Probably until he died.

Dawkins knew he couldn't let that happen.

He had to get the hell out of here.

But how?

First things first. He took stock of his physical condition. He moved both legs and while his left thigh was extremely sore, probably from a couple of good swift kicks from a boot, everything else seemed okay.

He moved both arms, first by bending the elbows, and then the wrists. Everything hurt, but everything also functioned.

His neck was okay, and his face was painful and numb in parts.

So, while he wouldn't be winning any beauty contests at the moment, his physical condition wasn't horrible. Meaning, he could walk. And maybe even run a little bit.

But he had to get out.

Now.

While Darnell was gone.

Troy was sitting about eight feet away.

Dawkins considered the practicality of charging him. He'd have to roll off the cot, get to his feet and cover the distance before Troy could pick up the rifle, point it at him, and shoot him. Check that, it was a lever-action gun, so Troy would have to pick it up, work the lever, then aim and shoot.

The question was, how would his body react? Could he vault from the cot and land on his feet?

Doubtful.

If he tipped over, fell onto the floor, pushed up with his hands and charged, he guessed it would take about a second and a half. Maybe two if he stumbled.

Too long.

He had to get Troy to come closer.

But how?

His stomach turned at the thought of another fight in this condition. He had beaten the three brothers when he was fresh and healthy.

Now, with his injuries, he knew he wouldn't win the next one.

He also realized that it wasn't just his emotions that were causing him to feel sick to his stomach.

It was blood.

He had probably swallowed a ton of it while he was unconscious.

And just like that, his plan came to him.

CHAPTER TWENTY-THREE

"I'm here about that table," Darnell said.

I looked from him to Harrison, who nodded and got to his feet.

"Good to meet you," Harrison said, and we shook hands. "Good luck on your project."

Harrison had that smile at the corner of his mouth and there was no doubt in my mind how much he was enjoying being in the know, and watching me fumble around in the dark.

Truth was, it pissed me off, but there was nothing I could do about it, for now.

I got outside and noticed Darnell's big red truck. It was one of those Hummer H3s, with the big knobby tires. It had seen better days, that was for sure.

It wasn't nearly as masculine as my minivan, which I climbed into, fired up and drove back to the resort in Good Isle. As I drove, I thought about how cool those big, knobby off-road tires would look on my minivan.

A trip to the auto department at Costco was in order when I got back to Grosse Pointe.

Anna, the girls and Ellen were all at the pool when I arrived back at the resort.

"Get your suit on," Anna told me.

"Show us your patented belly flop," Ellen suggested.

The girls were getting out of the water, though, so instead, I wrapped them up in towels and dried their hair.

"We're going back after we change," Anna said. "I booked you into a Super 8 just down the street where you can stay until Ellen solves your case for you."

My wife and my sister shared a laugh at my expense.

Anna sometimes acted as my travel agent when I needed a hand, like now, when the free stay was ending.

"What's your plan?" I asked Ellen.

"Not sure yet," she said, pointing at her phone. "No word."

I nodded. "Why don't you stick around? I could use some backup while I finish this case."

"Are you close?" She raised an eyebrow, as if it was pointless to even ask.

"Let's go girls," Anna said, saving me from an answer. "These two are going to talk shop and we have to pack. I want to get home before rush hour traffic."

I hugged the girls and Anna, and they walked out of the pool area, leaving wet footprints behind them.

Ellen and I left, too. We found the dining room empty and grabbed a table with four chairs. The only people in the place were a couple of servers setting up tables. A giant black bear, stuffed of course, stood in the corner and supervised all of us. I wondered if, at night when all the guests were asleep, the stuffed bear chased the stuffed moose around the resort. Maybe they were friends and played in the pool.

"So how's the search for Dynamite going?" Ellen asked, interrupting my musings.

I took her through everything I'd done, including the meetings with Don White and John Harrison.

"Huh," she said. "So, you're nowhere."

"More or less," I said. "No way to ID the guy driving Dynamite's Bronco. No one's seen him. He hasn't reappeared."

"This is a lot tougher gig for you when you don't have a sibling on the local police force, isn't it?" Ellen asked.

"Don't flatter yourself," I said. But she was right, of course.

"Now what are you going to do?"

"I need more information," I said. "Something more to go on. It happens almost every time I take a case like this. I have to go back to my client and see if there's anything else they can tell me."

"And do they usually have something else to say?"

I winked at her.

"Here's a little tip from an experienced private investigator regarding clients," I said. "They *always* have more information."

CHAPTER TWENTY-FOUR

The next morning, I checked out of the resort, saw my family off, and got a rental car from the local Avis dealer.

It was a real piece of crap.

A tiny white Chevy with an engine that sounded like a lawn mower.

It was time to talk to my client.

Lindsey Nordegren and her absentee husband did not live in one of the mega mansions along the shore of Lake Michigan.

Instead, they lived in a newly built contemporary dwelling on a bluff overlooking a small inland lake, about a mile from Good Isle.

I turned down a road named Nordegren Way and it led to only one house.

First clue you have a lot of money? When you can name the street you live on after yourself.

I could see it now: John Rockne Road. Boy, that sounded nice.

The house was a concrete monster, all right angles, over-hangs, towering windows and exposed black metal supports.

A monument to modernism, new home construction, and an unlimited budget.

It was also nearly entirely devoid of landscaping save for perfectly manicured green grass that ran down to a dock that stuck out into the breathtakingly blue water of the lake.

Lindsey Nordegren was waiting for me at the front door.

"Leif is very big into security," she explained. "I've been watching you for the past five minutes."

My first reaction was to think if I'd done something gross. Luckily, I hadn't.

Lindsey gestured for me to enter the house, so I complied. Black metal steps led up to a wide open space that served as a great room. It was like still being outside thanks to the banks of windows that made up practically every wall in the room. The floor was wood, as blonde as the lady of the house, and all of the walls were painted white.

It felt a little like an insane asylum. Or, at least, what I thought one would look like.

We crossed the room, Lindsey's black heels making a sound that seemed deafening in the quiet space.

She gestured to a sitting area whose window provided a stunning view of the lake.

"This lake is amazing," I said. "The water looks like the Caribbean."

"Spring-fed," Lindsey said. "It's the only thing I liked about the place."

"Really? It's spectacular." I had caught her use of the past tense but decided to let it go. For now.

"It's for sale if you want to buy it," she replied.

I thought about how to respond to that.

"It includes the lake," she added.

At first, I thought she was joking, but then when I looked at her face, I realized she was serious. And I also realized why the lake looked so gorgeous. There weren't any other homes on it. The whole lake to myself. How cool would that be?

"Do you go skinny dipping every night?" I asked. "I would."

She looked out at the lake and I thought she was going to say something, but then she changed her mind.

Lindsey turned from the window and looked at me, her eyes cool and distant.

"I take it you haven't found him," she said.

"I'm afraid you're right," I admitted.

She sighed.

"It would have been nice to get this all wrapped up," she said.

Sometimes I had to admit I could be a little slow on the uptake. Saying the house was for sale, the emptiness of the place.

"You're leaving," I said.

"It seems to be a trend." There was irony in her voice, along with sadness and resignation.

"Your husband isn't coming back, is he?" I had finally put it all together.

"No, it seems he has fallen in love with Italy. Specifically, an Italian countess with almost as much money as Leif," she said. "Their relationship, I'm sure, is just an embarrassment of riches."

Now the house felt really big and empty. I felt sorry for her.

"Where are you going?"

"Anywhere but Italy," she said with a laugh. God, she was a beautiful woman. With the startling blue of the lake behind her, her face was like a perfect sculpture. And when she smiled, it only got prettier.

"Somewhere warm," she continued. "It's been so cold up

here. I've always liked San Diego. Maybe I'll get a condo in La Jolla. Stare out at the Pacific instead of Lake Nordegren."

The laugh was more of a scoff.

"Do you want me to keep looking for Dawkins?"

She took her time answering. Was she considering how much of an investment she had made emotionally in him? I figured there would be a direct correlation between her true feelings for Dawkins and the lengths she would go to find him.

Finally, she reached her answer.

"I want you to find him," she said. "Cost is no object. You can continue to get your checks from Beau, although now that Leif and I are officially over, there's not much need for secrecy. But it will make things easier."

I assumed she meant in the impending divorce.

"Okay," I said. "Is there anything more you can tell me about Dawkins? I know we've been through it all once. But since then, have you thought of any other places he might have gone? Or been taken? Anybody want to hurt him that you didn't want to discuss in front of Beau, or that maybe you realized you'd neglected to mention?"

"No, we didn't do a whole lot of talking when we were together," she said, raising her eyebrow slightly at me.

"He had some business issues with his former manager and the manager's company," I offered.

"Don White?" she asked. "It wouldn't surprise me. That guy is a creep. One time I came home and he was here, talking to my husband. Pitching some kind of business deal or something. After he left, I told Leif I never wanted to see that man in my home again. Gave me the willies."

"And Dynamite had no family you knew of?"

"He never mentioned anyone," Lindsey said. "He hardly mentioned anyone or anything because he's a man of few words. Very thoughtful, though. Just doesn't often share what's on his mind. I liked that about him."

"Well, as a PI trying to track him down, I definitely *don't* like that about him," I said. "I like loud, obnoxious people. The quiet ones make my job a lot harder."

She shrugged her shoulders and I knew what she was thinking.

What can you do?

We talked a little more but she had nothing to add, and I got the sense she wasn't too happy to have a visitor. Eventually, she walked me to the front door and we said our goodbyes.

When I drove away from the house, I glanced back and she was framed in the middle of the house's main window.

It looked like a staged photograph.

A sad one.

CHAPTER TWENTY-FIVE

Ever-widening circles.

That's what the good guys in the old Westerns would do. If they were tracking a bad guy, and they lost the trail, they'd slowly ride in ever-widening circles, looking for any stray track or sign that their quarry had passed through.

Not exactly the highest tech approach to finding a missing person, but Good Isle was a small town. And as long as I believed that Dynamite Dawkins was still in the general area, I figured *what the hell*.

A vintage Bronco would stand out like a sore thumb, even up here.

There were old SUVs, certainly, but most of them were ridden hard and put away wet, as the saying goes. With all the snow, the roads during winter were doused heavily with salt, and if you lived long enough up here you could tell by the giant swatches of rust your vehicle soon became infected with.

So that's what I did.

I drove into the center of town, and then slowly drove in a

rough circle, widening my search area with each turn. I was mostly looking for the Bronco, even though I'd done my homework and had looked at enough pictures of Dawkins to know what he looked like.

But the Bronco was the key.

A fully restored, mint condition, vintage Ford Bronco would be easy to spot.

And once I had the vehicle, I was pretty sure I would have Dawkins.

I quickly learned that there were no real bad areas of Good Isle. If Ellen got the job here, she wouldn't have too much crime to deal with. Not even littering.

It also became apparent that despite a general sense of sophistication, the citizens of Good Isle liked to drink. There seemed to be more than enough drinking establishments to go around. Which meant the opposite for Ellen. Probably a lot of drunk and disorderlies up here, especially during the winter when there was nothing else to do but get hammered.

As the saying went, during winter, it wasn't just the streets that got plowed daily.

On one of the last roads on the outskirts of Good Isle I saw a Bronco and allowed my hopes to momentarily spike. But when I got closer, I saw that it was a disaster on wheels with no hubcaps, covered in rust, and mismatched body panels.

No way that was a "lovingly restored" Bronco.

Another hour took me out further and further into the country, where my circles always eventually touched back to the lake.

My gas tank indicator told me I needed to fill up and it was good timing because I was sick of driving, but then a big white SUV roared past me. It was a high-end Japanese model, maybe a Lexus or an Infiniti.

It wasn't the make of the vehicle that caught my eye.

It was the driver.

Don White.

Forgetting the need to get gas, I set off in pursuit.

He was driving way too fast for the posted speed limit, which was 45.

White was doing at least seventy and I had to wonder where the hell he was going that demanded such a fast pace.

We were going directly east, away from Lake Michigan, out toward some of the other smaller, inland lakes, and eventually the Interstate.

About a mile from I-75, White suddenly braked and took a crazy-fast left turn onto a small dirt road.

Now my yellow warning light for low gas came on, but I had to follow. I could always hitchhike if I ran out of fuel.

The road was steep and covered in gravel. Remnants of White's dust obscured my view as I desperately tried to keep up, but I knew I was falling further and further behind.

If only I had the minivan. Yeah, say what you want, but that vehicle had a nice V-6, very powerful. Plus, I sat up higher, which would have helped with all this dust.

Instead, I was in a glorified golf cart with an engine that sounded like an oven fan, so low to the ground I was in the thickest part of the dirt cloud.

I was about to stop and turn around when suddenly, there was Don White's big SUV, in the middle of the road, turned sideways blocking the way.

Even with my foot jammed on the brake, I was barely able to stop, the car sliding forward until I was a foot from smashing into the bigger vehicle.

The door handle was in my grasp when it was wrenched open and my arm was grabbed.

Suddenly, I was hauled bodily from the car and as I straightened up, a fist crashed into my jaw.

My back landed on the road and I looked up to see a man now standing above me.

I'd seen him before.

In John Harrison's shop.

What was his name?

Darnell.

CHAPTER TWENTY-SIX

The sucker punch that had knocked me on my ass, hadn't knocked me out.

However, the sequence of events that landed me in the back of Don White's SUV was like a bad movie, thanks in no small part to the effects of the blow.

My mind was suddenly grainy, full of poorly edited jump cuts and a bizarre soundtrack.

The punch had been a good one and my face ached. I had a horrible headache and being crammed into the back of the SUV wasn't helping matters.

My hands were tied behind my back and my face was smashed into the floor. I rolled over as best I could, until I could at least see the ceiling of the vehicle.

Yep, definitely Don White's SUV. I could see the back of the seat to my right, it looked like plush leather and I also got a whiff of cologne. Of course, Don White would wear a ton of cologne. The man blasted shotguns in his backyard wearing a thong.

Shit.

I thought about my rental car. What were they going to do with it? And my phone. Where was my phone? I tried to feel if it was in my pocket and I didn't think so. I thought back and figured that I had probably set it in the car's cupholder.

Not good.

The rental car had a GPS, though. So I figured if Ellen would wonder where I was, she might go there and see if I'd returned the car, at which point they would be able to find the vehicle.

But how long would all of that take?

Plus, that would only happen if my abductors hadn't stolen the car, which they probably had. After assault and kidnapping, what was a little grand theft auto?

Or maybe they'd drive it into a lake somewhere after stuffing my dead body into it.

That's real positive, John.

I started sweating and could make out voices from the front of the vehicle. They probably didn't have the air conditioning turned on for the back of the vehicle.

"Hey, can you turn on the AC back here?" I shouted, glad they hadn't gagged me.

"Shut the fuck up," a voice called back. "Say anything else and we'll put a bullet in your head and dump you in the swamp."

He sounded sincere, but technically there weren't any swamps around here. Marshes, for sure. But no one thought of them as swamps. I made a mental note to correct him once my imposed period of silence was over.

That had sounded like Don White's voice, but I couldn't be sure. My ears were ringing from being socked in the jaw.

As we drove, I occasionally heard snippets of conversation from the front.

"...bullshit..."

"...how many..."

"...ass-kicking..."

"...bitch..."

Not exactly the Algonquin Round Table going on up there, I thought.

But both the tone and the content of their words confirmed that White and Darnell, and probably others, had grabbed Dawkins, too.

Was John Harrison involved?

Darnell had been at his shop. Was this some kind of militia thing? Why would they have grabbed a retired boxer? Ransom? Demands from the government?

Maybe the plan was to blackmail Lindsay Nordegren. I would be more than happy to tell them what a bad plan that was.

The whole thing didn't make any sense to me.

Right now, I wished I was on the way back to Grosse Pointe with my family, instead of going who knows where in Don White's gaudy vehicle.

After what felt like hours but was probably more likely forty-five minutes or so, we hit a really rough road, and I knew we were going into the middle of nowhere. Roads like these are all over northern Michigan and when you feel that washboard pattern, you know you're well away from modern civilization.

Eventually, the vehicle came to a stop. My circulation had stopped well before that, and my fingers and hands were tingling from numbness.

The passengers in the front got out and I hoped they were coming to get me, but they weren't.

I waited another twenty minutes before the rear door opened and Darnell hoisted me out.

My legs had turned into jelly so I stumbled and nearly fell.

In front of me was a temporary tent, with a square in the middle delineated by a single strand of rope shaped roughly into a square.

A boxing ring.

CHAPTER TWENTY-SEVEN

Dawkins started with a small cough.

Troy had Wheel of Fortune on the television and was shouting out guesses.

"Green beans!" he yelled.

Dawkins coughed again, this time a little louder.

"Great plans?" Troy shouted. "Shit!"

Billy had been working himself up, swallowing as much saliva and air as possible, psyching himself up for what he was about to do next.

Troy helped by shutting off the television after the contestants guessed the answer before he did.

Never a good sign of your intelligence.

"Stupid show," Troy said. "But I'd bang the crap out of Vanna, even if she's eighty years old. Instead of turning those letters she can twirl my balls."

Dawkins suddenly buckled on the cot, as if wracked by a spasm.

He rolled onto his side and willed himself to vomit, sending a shower of saliva mixed with blood onto the floor of the cabin.

"Christ, what now, you damn loser," Troy said. "Gross. What the hell?"

Dawkins sneaked a peek up at him, saw him stand up, the rifle still leaning against the side of the chair.

Step one, Dawkins thought. Separate him from his weapon.

"What a mess you are, you dumb sonofabitch," Troy continued. "I oughta kick your face in. Prize fighter my white ass."

Dawkins forced himself to heave again and this time he sent a spew of bloody mucus onto Troy's boots.

"Shit!" Troy yelled. He came closer and did what Dawkins was hoping he would do. He kicked him in the stomach.

The problem for Troy was, Billy arms were cuffed in front of him, so the blow came directly into his hands.

Dawkins responded by grabbing ahold of Troy's leg and corkscrewing his body, placing a huge amount of torque on the leg and Dawkins heard Troy's knee pop.

Troy lost his balance, fell and landed on his back.

"Help!" Troy yelled, high-pitched and in a panic.

Dawkins was immediately on top of him.

He put his hands together to form one fist and then he twisted to the right and brought them down together, like swinging a baseball bat. His double-fisted blow caught Troy on the chin and drove his head back onto the wood floor.

Dawkins repeated the punch three more times until Troy's jaw was hanging crookedly by a single hinge and his eyes were rolled back completely in his head.

Troy was out of the game, and maybe even dead.

Dawkins pivoted off of Troy and dug through the man's pants for the handcuff key. He found it in the right pocket, and carefully unlocked the cuffs. He stood, a little unsteady, and retrieved the rifle.

He wasn't a big gun guy, but he had shot before.

There were keys on the kitchen counter and Billy grabbed them. He stopped for a water bottle and drank deeply. He was half-tempted to go into the bathroom and check his face but decided against it.

He had to move.

Dawkins went back to Troy and dug through his other pocket looking for a cell phone. It wasn't there. He went back to the chair, noticed a jean jacket on the floor. An inside pocket revealed Troy's phone.

Dawkins put the phone in his pocket and crossed the room to the front of the cabin. There were no windows looking out so he wasn't sure what he would be walking into. But he'd rather get outside, get into a vehicle and get the hell out of here, than stay in the cabin and call the cops.

He opened the door.

Darnell's gun was pointed directly at his face.

"Great timing there, Dynamite."

CHAPTER TWENTY-EIGHT

I saw a man emerge from the tiny structure to the right of the makeshift tent and boxing ring.

Behind him was Darnell, with a huge silver revolver that looked like a small cannon.

The man walking in front, I recognized.

Despite the face that looked like it had been beaten bloody, Billy "Dynamite" Dawkins had arrived.

It was hard to believe it was actually him.

One of the most legendary fighters of all time, out here, in the sticks.

He was a little smaller than I imagined, a little older, but he was still impressive. Lean, with a narrow waist and broad shoulders. Even though it looked like he'd had the crap knocked out of him, he had a presence. A look that was probably very effective at intimidating wannabes.

"What the fuck is all this?" Don White said, looking at the makeshift boxing ring. "Jesus Christ, you were supposed to kill him. What the hell is this?"

"No harm in making a little money while we got ready to get rid of this little bitch," Darnell said. "He just beat the shit out of Troy inside. Might have killed him. Damn, you gotta keep your eye on him."

"Redneck, white trash, dumb shit," Don White said.

"What'd you say?" Darnell snapped back.

"You heard me." Don White turned to me. "Now we've got this asshole to worry about, too. We're going to have to get rid of them both."

White turned to me.

"It was that bitch, right? Nordegren?"

He turned to Dawkins.

"You were banging her, huh? Nice work, Billy. You were always good with the ladies."

"Fuck you, Don," Dawkins said. "That's what this is about?"

"Sort of," Don White said. "I owed some money to that bitch's hubby. If I did this thing for him, my debt was wiped clean. A great arrangement until this fucking hillbilly didn't just get rid of you like he was supposed to."

White gestured toward me.

"Okay, it's over. Take this one," he said, and pointed at me. And then he pointed at Dawkins. "And that one and get rid of them both."

Overhead, a bird flew by and it was big. A raven, or maybe an eagle. Was it a sign? Some clouds had moved in and now the clearing was bathed in shadow.

I knew I didn't want to die here. My eyes found Dawkins and we looked at each other. It was time to make some kind of move, his expression told me. He had a gun pointed at the back of his head.

"I don't like your tone," Darnell said. "Matter of fact, it kinda pisses me off."

Don White looked like he was going to explode.

"My tone? Fuck my tone, you inbred piece of shit."

Another bird flew up from behind me and I judged the

distance between myself and Don White. It would take me at least three steps to get to him.

Before I could make my move I sensed movement from Darnell.

He had swung the revolver from behind Dawkins's head so that it was now pointing at Don White.

"No!" I said, and dove toward White's legs.

I was too late.

The big revolver erupted and Don White fell backward, landing next to me on the ground.

Not all of him made the trip, though, because half of his head was gone.

For a moment, the silence hung in the air.

I rolled over and got to my feet, looked down at what was left of Don White, and then up at Billy Dawkins.

"You don't call me white trash," Darnell said, looking at the deceased body of Don White. "When you do that, you insult not just me but all of my kin. And that, I just can't accept."

It was time to make a move. Any kind of move.

I put my hands out in front of me and took a step toward Darnell.

"Let's just–"

A gunshot rang out, and I jumped back, putting my hands to my chest. Had Darnell shot me?

He couldn't have because–

Darnell toppled over, his big gun landing in the dirt three feet from Dynamite Dawkins.

It was then I realized the sound had come from behind me. From where the birds had kept taking flight.

Now I knew why.

I turned, just in time to see John Harrison and three men, all in camouflage, walking up to the clearing.

"Thought I might find you here," Harrison said to me as he walked past.

The other men walked past me like I wasn't even there.

One of them went into the cabin and returned with some keys.

"Troy's dead," he said.

The other man opened the door to one of the big aluminum sheds.

Inside, I saw a vintage Ford Bronco.

Harrison gestured for me to join him next to Dawkins and his other men. I tried not to look down at what was left of Darnell.

It wasn't pretty.

"A friend of Mr. Dawkins asked me to keep an ear out," Harrison said. "I knew Darnell was up to something, but I will admit even this surprised me. However, Darnell is an associate of mine and we have some private business that needs to remain private."

"We have to call the cops," I said. "There are three dead men here."

Harrison looked at me. All of the easygoing charm vanished.

"My advice to you is to go back to Grosse Pointe the first chance you get. Because the first chance is your last chance. This was simply a criminal enterprise gone wrong."

One of Harrison's men was carefully placing a gun in Don White's dead hand, making sure White's fingerprints were all over the weapon.

Harrison pointed at White. "He and Darnell had a shootout, after Darnell killed Troy."

He held out his hand and one of his men handed him a set of keys.

Harrison tossed them to Dynamite.

"Take your Bronco, which is a very fine ride, I might add," he said. "Take it, and him with you," he said, pointing at me. "Go back to Good Isle and forget all about this, okay? We'll make sure there's no sign of you in the cabin. We'll take care of these two." He pointed toward Don White's big, luxury SUV. "And that."

Dawkins didn't say a word, just turned and started walking toward the Bronco.

Harrison turned to me.

"Better hurry, Mr. Rockne," he said. "Your ride is leaving."

CHAPTER TWENTY-NINE

"I think we should go straight to the ER," I said to Dynamite Dawkins.

Dawkins looked at me out of the corner of his bruised and scary-looking eye. His face was swollen, his lips were split, and there was blood all over the front of his clothing.

"I don't think so," he said. "What would we tell them? I fell down the stairs?"

It didn't seem like a good idea to argue with the man. Especially since I knew that even in his current physical state, he could kick my ass all the way into Wisconsin.

He opened a compartment between us and looked inside.

"Huh," he said.

It was his phone.

He checked to see if it had power but it didn't.

Dawkins reached into his pocket, and found another phone. As he drove, he wiped it clean with the tail of his shirt, and then held it carefully with the fabric, rolled down his window and tossed it.

"Troy's," he said, by way of explanation.

There was a power cord with an adapter for the cigarette lighter, so he plugged in his own phone and it beeped, showing it was starting to charge.

We drove down the bumpy country road until we came to an intersection where the cross street was paved.

Without a word, we turned to the west, knowing eventually we'd hit Lake Michigan.

"Who are you?" he asked, finally.

"John Rockne," I said. "Lindsey Nordegren hired me to find you. I'm a private investigator."

"She was worried about me?" he asked. A small smile tugged at the corner of his swollen and bloody mouth.

"Yes," I said. "She told me to find you. No matter what it took."

"She's a woman not easily discouraged," he said.

Moments later, we pulled up to another cross street.

"Ah, I know where we are," he said.

He took that turn, and suddenly, his phone came to life.

"Do you mind if I make a quick phone call?" I said. "When they grabbed me, they got my phone, too."

"Go ahead," he said. "I never drive and text."

I was about to punch in Ellen's phone number but then I stopped.

"Um, where are we going?" I asked.

"I'm going home."

"Okay."

This time I didn't hesitate and I punched in Ellen's phone number.

"Hey, it's me. Can you meet me at Dynamite, I mean, Mr. Dawkins's house?"

She wanted to know when.

"How long before we get there?" I asked my driver.

"Twenty minutes, give or take," he said.

"Twenty minutes, give or take," I told Ellen.

She said she'd heard him.

I disconnected from the call and put the phone back in its holder.

"You have a beautiful house, by the way," I said.

I got the stink eye from the bruised eye.

"Lindsey gave us the key," I said quickly. "She was very worried about you."

Dynamite didn't seem to want to talk, so I occupied myself by looking out the window at Michigan's rolling hills, and admiring the quality of the restoration my driver had done on his vehicle. Everything looked original. The leather upholstery. The dashboard. It was like being transported to my childhood thirty years ago.

The urge to talk came to me, but I sensed my companion wasn't in the mood for chit chat.

I also thought about the fact that I had just witnessed two men being killed, and I hadn't called the police.

Failing to report something like that was highly illegal and would certainly cost me my license and my livelihood. I didn't know what Harrison's plan was. I didn't even know what township that cabin technically belonged to. We were way outside of Good Isle's city limits, so I knew if the cops did get involved, they wouldn't be from Good Isle, which made me feel a sense of relief. I still didn't know what was going on with Ellen, but a triple murder wouldn't be a good way to start a new job.

Still, it made me more than a little uneasy not to go to the authorities. John Harrison, despite the charismatic charm, wasn't messing around. And I had a feeling if I went telling tales out of school, I might get a visit from him.

Plus, Don White was a bad guy, as was Darnell.

Additionally, all evidence would no doubt be destroyed

soon, if not already. If I went to the cops, and I somehow managed to lead them to the clearing, what would they find?

Either a carefully staged crime scene, or a whole lot of nothing.

No, my plan was to keep my mouth shut, and head back to Grosse Pointe as fast as possible.

CHAPTER THIRTY

Ellen was parked in front of Dynamite's house with my rental car intact.

We pulled into the driveway and Ellen walked over, handed me my cell phone.

"Rental car company's GPS worked," she said.

Dawkins came around the other side of the Bronco and stopped when he saw Ellen. Ellen looked at him with an odd expression.

"You look terrible," she said.

Dawkins smiled, and for the first time I realized what a handsome man he was. Maybe that's why Ellen had looked at him so strangely.

"I clean up well," he said. "Which is what I'm going to do right now. And sleep."

He went into the house and I followed Ellen to my rental car.

I let her drive and I started to fill her in on what happened.

"Wait!" she said. "Were any laws broken?"

"Uh, yeah, there was—"

"Stop! They offered me the job and I took it," she said. "I can't hear about anything illegal or I'll have to investigate."

"But you haven't started yet."

"Doesn't matter."

"Oh."

It sort of hit me out of the blue.

"Holy shit! You got the job! Congratulations," I said.

"Thanks." My sister seemed incredibly happy and actually smiled at me, a feat that I hadn't seen accomplished in so long I assumed it was a physical impossibility.

"Christ, I can't believe you're going to leave Grosse Pointe," I said. "You won't be around. You're going to miss me so much."

Ellen gave me a smirk.

"I kind of surprised myself," she said. "The longer I was here, the more it felt right to me. I think it's a good opportunity, and I was getting tired of Grosse Pointe. It will be nice to have some new challenges."

It started to sink in. I felt sad, but wasn't about to admit that. I hated it when people got mushy.

Instead, I focused on the reaction Ellen and Dawkins had shared.

"I have a feeling the first community involvement project will be stopping by Dynamite's place," I said. "I saw the way you looked at him and the way he looked at you."

"Shut up, John."

"I hope the forests up here aren't dry because the sparks were clearly flying."

She ignored me and pulled into the parking lot of the hotel.

We were going to grab our respective suitcases, pack up, and then she would follow me back to the car rental place.

Once I'd returned it, she'd give me a ride back to Grosse Pointe.

Home for me.

A new adventure for Ellen.

Do you want more killer crime fiction, along with the chance to win free books? Then sign up for the DAN AMES NEWSLETTER:

For special offers and new releases, sign up here

ALSO BY DAN AMES

DEAD WOOD (John Rockne Mystery #1)

HARD ROCK (John Rockne Mystery #2)

COLD JADE (John Rockne Mystery #3)

LONG SHOT (John Rockne Mystery #4)

EASY PREY (John Rockne Mystery #5)

BODY BLOW (John Rockne Mystery #6)

THE KILLING LEAGUE (Wallace Mack Thriller #1)

THE MURDER STORE (Wallace Mack Thriller #2)

FINDERS KILLERS (Wallace Mack Thriller #3)

DEATH BY SARCASM (Mary Cooper Mystery #1)

MURDER WITH SARCASTIC INTENT (Mary Cooper Mystery #2)

GROSS SARCASTIC HOMICIDE (Mary Cooper Mystery #3)

KILLER GROOVE (Rockne & Cooper Mystery #1)

BEER MONEY (Burr Ashland Mystery #1)

THE CIRCUIT RIDER (Circuit Rider #1)

KILLER'S DRAW (Circuit Rider #2)

TO FIND A MOUNTAIN (A WWII Thriller)

ABOUT THE AUTHOR

Dan Ames is a USA TODAY bestselling author and winner of the Independent Book Award for Crime Fiction. You can learn more about him at AuthorDanAmes.com

www.authordanames.com
dan@authordanames.com

Made in the USA
Monee, IL
09 March 2021

62345628R00090